'I want us

There was a sho... ...at him, then A... 'That's a...novel idea.'

'But an entirely logical one,' Garson said. 'I'd like to bring Oliver more closely into my family. Oliver will also benefit from having a man around the place. The child-care manuals would insist that I'd provide a steadying influence, a role model and help make him rounded as a person.'

She flashed him a brittle glance. 'You've been doing your homework.'

'If we get married I'll also look after Oliver financially,' he continued, 'and look after you.'

Anya's backbone stiffened. 'No, thanks; I'm not being bought!'

Elizabeth Oldfield's writing career started as a teenage hobby, when she had articles published. However, on her marriage the creative instinct was diverted into the production of a daughter and son. A decade later, when her husband's job took them to Singapore, she resumed writing and had her first romance accepted in 1982. Now hooked on the genre, she produces an average of three books a year. They live in London, and Elizabeth travels widely to authenticate the background of her books.

Recent titles by the same author:

FAST AND LOOSE

INTIMATE RELATIONS

BY
ELIZABETH OLDFIELD

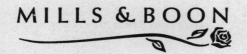

MILLS & BOON

*MILLS & BOON and the Rose Device
are trademarks of the publisher.
Harlequin Mills & Boon Limited,
Eton House, 18-24 Paradise Road, Richmond, Surrey TW9 1SR*

© Elizabeth Oldfield 1996

ISBN 0 263 79577 2

*Set in Times Roman 10 on 11½ pt.
01-9608-54057 C1*

Made and printed in Great Britain

CHAPTER ONE

THE old superstition was true—bad luck *did* strike in runs of three, Anya thought ruefully—for yesterday she had been walloped by a trio of what, to her, seemed like calamities.

Pushing her foot down on the accelerator, she coaxed her geriatric Volkswagen to increase its speed and as it settled into its maximum, a trundling fifty, she began to brood.

First, she had received a letter from her major customer advising her that, due to the current slump in trade, they were closing a couple of their shops; which robbed her of two outlets. Anya frowned at the spring-green hedges which edged the winding country lane. This morning she intended to replace those outlets, yet they would still be a loss and she could ill afford to lose business.

Second, when she had collected Oliver from school, his teacher had told her that he had got into an uncharacteristic and astonishingly fierce fight with another little boy and couldn't—or wouldn't—say why.

And, third, when Roger Adlam had deposited her at her gate after the village inn's monthly quiz night, he had snaked a lecherous arm around her, yanked her close and kissed her. Anya grimaced. Despite her protests that all she wanted was for them to be friends, platonic friends, might the sleek-haired young farmer attempt to kiss her again? She hoped not. She hoped he would not start to pressurise.

But there was no time to fret about the local Casanova now. She must concentrate on this morning's appointments and how she was going to persuade the gift-shop owners to stock her goods. Fleetingly Anya's gaze dipped to her cream georgette blouse and slim-fitting black leather trousers. As well as having made up her face with special care—mushroom eyeshadow, a touch of blusher, rosy lip-gloss—she was wearing what she privately termed her 'sock it to 'em' outfit and hopefully her appearance, plus an earnest spiel about the value and marketability of her dried-flower specialities, should—

As she rounded a corner, Anya blinked. Just a few yards ahead, a plump brown-speckled hen pheasant was promenading like a cheer-leader straight towards her. 'Move!' she yelled, and when it took no notice she swerved frantically to the other side of the narrow road. 'Help!' she shrieked, for she was hurtling off the road, through a fortuitously placed opening to a field and ploughing into a jungle of high ferns. Behind her, the pheasant continued to high-step serenely on its way.

Clutching at the steering wheel, Anya stamped down hard on the brake. There was a second erratic swerve, a bone-jarring series of judders as she ricocheted from one sneakily hidden boulder and against another, then the car slewed to a halt. Fortunately, for ahead she had glimpsed the sparkle of water. Cutting the engine, Anya drew in a shaky breath. The entire incident had lasted seconds, yet it took a full minute before she summoned up the strength to release her seat belt.

Fearfully, she turned. The back of the Beetle was filled with boxes of garlands, candleholder posies, bookmarks et cetera, but—praise be—her tight-wedged packing had kept them safe from harm, and whilst the flower arrangements in the luggage pit had suffered a few broken grasses they could be easily fixed. But what about her car?

Anya clambered out and, on jelly legs, walked around to the front. Dismay crashed over her in cold waves. The wing looked as if it had been beaten by a maniac with a sledgehammer and there were dents on both the door and rear panel. Repair bills were destined to be sizeable.

'Oh, no!' she wailed.

Tears threatened and for a moment Anya was tempted to sink to her knees and *sob*, but then her shoulders were straightened. She did not have too much time and, right now, her priority must be to mend those dried-flower arrangements. With what? she wondered, and peered ahead. The water which had sparkled was a sunlit pond. It lay in a tranquil hollow, overhung with trees and edged by reeds which grew in tall thickets.

Anya made her way down to the reeds and began to gather a selection. Spotting a particularly suitable honey-coloured bunch, she stepped closer to the water and crouched. She was in the process of deciding which stems to break off when a stone whizzed past her ear and crashed with a plonk into the pond, right in front of her.

'Eee-oww!' she gasped as plumes of water sprayed into the air, subjecting her to a cold and impromptu shower.

Anya struggled upright. Strands of sodden russet-brown hair hung over her eyes in a dripping curtain, trickles ran down her cheeks, her clothes were spattered with damply spreading circles. Minutes earlier she had been tempted to sob, but now she wanted to *scream*. And jump up and down in a frenzy. And punch things. Hard. She swiped the wet hair back from her brow. The jay-walking pheasant might have got clean away after committing its crime, but, she vowed furiously, the stone-thrower would not.

Anya swivelled. Her gaze narrowed. Off to one side and on the bank beyond the rushes stood a dark-haired man in a charcoal-grey suit. He was tall, well over six feet, with broad flat shoulders and lean hips. He had a strong jaw, fine-chiselled straight nose and a full mouth. She frowned. She had expected the culprit to be a child or some scruffy adolescent, not a suave business executive who, at a guess, was in his mid-thirties.

Her fingers curling tight around the reeds which she had gathered, and bent on denunciation, Anya stalked forward. Her progress was regal, until a drip formed at the end of her nose and she needed to back-hand it away. Then wet collected like grease on her chin and that had to be smeared off too. As she approached, her frown hardened into a glare. Instead of looking meekly repentant and subdued as his sin demanded, the man appeared to be fighting against amusement. His eyes had crinkled at the corners and his mouth was twitching.

Anya's hackles rose. How dared he? On another day and in another mood, she might have conceded that there was something comical about her hoity-toity drowned rat image, too, but coming after her near miss with the pheasant and the damage to her car his barely concealed grin was an insult. An infuriating impertinence.

'I'm very sorry,' he said as she marched up to confront him.

'So you damn well should be!' Anya snapped. 'And it isn't funny.'

His blue eyes sobered and his mouth was schooled. 'No, no, not at all,' the man agreed, and bowed a courteous head. 'Please forgive me.'

She glowered. He might look dutifully apologetic, yet there had been something in the mellifluous, liquorice-dark baritone which hinted at continuing humour. So

was he apologising for dousing her or merely for his urge
to laugh?

'It never occurred to you that throwing stones when
there are other people around is stupid and infantile and
dangerous?' Anya demanded, castigating him with each
word. 'Or don't you care?'

'I care,' he responded, and there was no humour now,
just firm assertion. 'However, I believed I was all alone.'

She gave a derisive grunt. Who was he trying to kid?
'You must've heard me arrive,' she declared, and swung
a hand to where the pale blue roof of the Volkswagen
was visible amongst the ferns. 'I hit a couple of boulders,
hard,' Anya said, with a frown. 'So how on earth you
could've missed the noise I can't imagine.'

'I missed it because I was on the telephone,' the man
told her.

'Telephone?'

'A portable. Inside my car. Over there,' he said, ges-
turing towards a gleaming black sports car which was
parked beyond a tree. 'How on earth you haven't noticed
it I can't imagine,' he murmured, when Anya looked at
the vehicle in wide-eyed surprise.

Her backbone stiffened. 'You could've killed me with
that stone,' she declared.

'Much as I hate to contradict a lady, I think not. It
may have created one heck of a splash, but it was little
more than a pebble.' He turned towards his car. 'I have
a towel; I'll get it for you.'

As the man strode away, the golden flecks sparked in
her hazel eyes. She did not appreciate his droll tit-for-
tat 'how on earth' nor the remark about hating to 'contradict a lady'. She had expected to receive, she *deserved*
to receive, shamefaced, humble and, yes, grovelling
apologies. Anya shot a resentful look at his broad back.

Though he did not seem the type who would grovel, no matter what crime he had committed.

Who was he? she wondered as the stone-thrower opened the boot of his car and started to unbuckle straps on a tan leather suitcase. After having lived in Lidden Magnor for almost four years, she was familiar with most of the people who dwelt in or who circulated around the small village, but she had not come across this individual before.

She studied him. His dark grey suit, slightly nipped at the waist, was impeccably tailored, his pristine white shirt looked custom-made, and his maroon tie had to be pure silk. The man's smart attire, allied with his patrician features and calm, self-assured manner—far too self-assured!—spoke of class with a capital C, so could he be a member of one of the old-money landowning families who lived in the noble mansions which dotted Dorset's hills and vales?

Perhaps, and yet he possessed an energy which suggested that rather than having been born with a silver spoon lodged comfortably in his well-shaped mouth he was a self-achiever who made his own way in the world. Her gaze swung to the gleaming sports car. And was making it with rip-roaring success. With deep-set blue eyes fringed by inky black lashes, the man had the kind of masculine good looks which could play havoc with the more easily impressed, Anya reflected.

She scowled. She was not impressed. Anything but. Though she felt certain that if she had seen him before she would have remembered.

'Thanks,' she said shortly, when the stranger returned to hand her a thick white towel.

Putting down the reeds, Anya started to rub her hair. Cut to shoulder-length and usually drawn back into a plait, this morning the russet curls had been worn loose.

Her aim had been to look film-star glamorous. Some chance now!

'Are you on holiday?' she enquired, curiosity getting the better of what she had intended to be a cold and condemning silence.

The man gave a twisted smile. 'If only,' he said, and slid his hands into his trouser pockets, his jacket flaring back. 'No, I have an appointment in this area, so I drove down straight from Heathrow.'

'You flew in earlier this morning?' Anya said, in surprise.

'My plane touched down at around seven a.m.,' he told her. 'From Indonesia. I'm back in England for a couple of days between business trips.'

She looked at him more closely. Whilst his clothes had survived amazingly well—though no doubt he'd travelled first class and a simpering stewardess would have tenderly hung up his jacket for him—there was a network of fine lines around his eyes and dark patches beneath them. The journey had taken its toll.

'A long-haul flight,' Anya remarked as she finger-combed the tousled mane of brown hair which, due to some brisk towelling, was almost dry, 'followed by— what, a two-hour drive?'

'Less than one and a half.' The man flicked a wry glance across at his car. 'That is a Maserati. I never sleep well on planes and I pulled off the road with the idea of grabbing some shut-eye,' he went on, 'but then I remembered a matter which I needed to speak to my secretary about, so—' His shoulders rose and fell.

'And after your phone call you decided to throw stones,' she accused, starting to blot at her trousers.

'I used to skim them when I was a kid and I had a sudden urge to see if I could skim them again,' he explained.

'But you couldn't,' Anya said tartly.

The man gave an apologetic grin. ''Fraid not, though that was my first try.'

'A disastrous try.' She frowned at the long sleeve of her blouse. The pond water had been brackenish and the splashes were leaving yellow stains on the pale georgette. 'I'm visiting several prospective clients this morning and I was hoping to wow them, but I shan't wow anyone looking like this.'

'On the contrary,' he said, with a quirk of a brow, 'if your clients are male and you turn up looking like you look now, I can assure you they'll be delighted.'

'Delighted?' Anya protested, and followed the dip of his eyes.

Her cheeks burned beet-red. Because she had been in a rush—making breakfast, running Oliver to school, loading her goods—body heat had kept her warm in the car. But a crisp April breeze was blowing and now her damp blouse was clinging to her breasts, outlining their high curves and her nipples, which, due to the chill, were erect, their points pronounced through the thin material. Yet why must he make such an embarrassingly personal comment? Anya longed to wither him with a retort of disdainful aplomb, but all aplomb had deserted her.

'You'll make their day. I'll pay for a new blouse,' the man carried on, without missing a beat, and, opening his jacket, he took a wallet from an inside pocket. There was no patting or digging around, just one fluid movement. 'Will a hundred pounds be enough?'

His offer was generous and would have been far more than enough, but Anya was too honest to take advantage.

'My blouse will dry-clean,' she told him.

'You're sure?' She nodded. 'Then I'll reimburse you for that,' he said, and handed her a twenty-pound note which, when she protested that it was too much, he insisted she must take. 'Everything OK now?' he asked, with an appealing grin.

On the point of giving a cool affirmative—he might have paid for his sins in cash but he had still wanted to laugh—Anya glanced at her wristwatch. 'No, because if I go home to change—' her voice rose in abrupt agitation '—I shall be late!'

'You can wear one of my shirts,' he said.

'Excuse me?'

'I had them laundered when I was in Jakarta, so they're clean. Come,' the man commanded, with a somewhat imperious flick of his fingers, and led her over to the Maserati where he produced three shirts from his suitcase. Neatly wrapped in Cellophane, one was lemon, one pale blue, one pink and white striped. 'If you roll up the sleeves and tuck the shirt loosely into your pants, you'll look fine.'

Aware of time passing, of how she prided herself on always being punctual, but also of how *intimate* the prospect of wearing the stranger's clothes seemed, Anya frowned. Yet he was right. The shirts were of such beautiful quality that, even though they were several sizes too big, her appearance would be acceptable. In fact, once her hair had been brushed, she would be back to being glamorous again.

'OK,' she said, and added a reluctant, 'Thanks.'

'Which?'

'The striped one,' she replied.

The man slid off the Cellophane and removed clips. A stiffening card was extracted, followed by a collar strip. Every action was adroit and swift.

'You must be a dab hand at crisis management,' Anya remarked drily.

'I have my moments. Take off your blouse,' he instructed.

Drooping the towel over the side of the boot, Anya started to unbutton a cuff. She had visualised retreating into her car to change, but his tone had been so matter-of-fact that it made scuttling off seem prim and girlishly coy. So did she disappear—or did she stay?

'I'm not your friendly neighbourhood rapist,' the man said, as if recognising her internal dilemma.

Anya gave a stiff smile. His good looks and lean physique meant he would never need to force himself on any female. Indeed, he probably spent a good proportion of his time fighting off unwelcome advances.

'I didn't think you were,' she replied.

'And you are wearing a bra. However,' he went on, 'even if you'd been *au naturel* I can assure you I wouldn't run amok, because I have seen a naked woman before.'

'More than one, I imagine,' Anya said pithily.

'The number must run into double digits,' he responded, then paused, frowning. 'Though you'd be surprised what a sheltered life I lead.'

The man shook out the shirt and Anya shed her blouse. Just as she would not scuttle off to her car, so she refused to turn away. Demonstrating that she could be just as matter-of-fact and urbane as he was seemed important. Besides, even if her white lace bra did dip low and even if her nipples remained noticeably and annoyingly pert she was still wearing as much as she would wear on a beach, she rationalised, if not a darn sight more.

Although her companion had vowed not to 'run amok', as she exchanged her blouse for the shirt Anya noticed that his gaze flickered down and, for a moment, he seemed fascinated by the silken swell of her breasts. Her pulse rate gave a sudden spurt. Adrenalin surged.

His interest made her feel pleased and...stimulated. Anya's brow crinkled. She did not usually respond in such a way towards strangers, handsome or otherwise. So how come he had affected her?

'Wait,' the man commanded as she started to push an arm into a shirtsleeve. 'Wet,' he explained, and, stepping forward, he started to towel-dry one shoulder.

Anya stood rigid. As he rubbed at her skin, he was close, so close. She told herself that the gesture was automatic, practical and meant nothing, yet with his straight dark brows lowered and his blue eyes intent he made it seem caring, like a lover's touch.

'Thanks,' she said, relieved when his towelling ended.

Anya drew on the shirt and fastened the buttons. The sleeves were rolled to her elbows and without undoing the zip of her trousers—which would have taken being matter-of-fact a little *too* far—she tucked in the shirt.

'It looks much better on you than it does on me,' the man said, and pulled a face. 'That makes me sound like such a smooth talker.'

Anya could not help a smile. 'And a clichéd one.'

'Guilty as charged,' he agreed, 'though in my defence I should point out that I'm jet-lagged.'

'Your defence is accepted,' she said.

He grinned. 'Thanks.'

'If you'll give me your name and address, I'll send your shirt back as soon as possible,' Anya continued.

'There's no rush,' the stranger said, and, opening his jacket and taking out his wallet again, he extracted an address card.

She gazed down at it. The black embossed script on the thick white gold-edged card revealed that he was called Garson Deverill and he lived in Chelsea. Fate might have conspired to bring them together in the depths of the Dorset countryside early on this April morning,

Anya thought wryly, yet his lifestyle in the expensive and trendy London enclave would be a million light years away from hers.

'What're you going to do with those?' Garson Deverill enquired, when, having slipped the card into her pocket and retrieved her blouse, she bent to gather up the bundle of reeds.

'Mend my flower arrangements. I sell them and I'm taking samples to show to gift shops,' Anya explained, 'but when I hit the boulders just now they were damaged.'

His gaze swung to the Volkswagen. 'And your car was damaged too,' he said, and went across with her to the vehicle. 'Hell,' he muttered. 'What happened?'

'I swerved to avoid a pheasant, lost control, and—'

'A pheasant?' he repeated.

'I came round a corner and there it was, right in front of me.'

'Are you one of those animal rights fanatics?' Garson Deverill demanded.

'No.'

'But you'd save a bird and sacrifice your own car?'

'What was I supposed to do—run over it?' Anya protested.

'If it didn't have the wit to fly away at the last moment, yes.'

She shuddered. 'I couldn't.'

'Whilst it may have escaped your attention, pheasants are not an endangered species,' Garson Deverill said drily. 'In fact, all over the country people are killing the damn things and serving them up for dinner, stuffed with sausage meat and garnished with sprigs of watercress.'

'Maybe, but the difference is that they kill them by shooting them, not by ironing them flat with cars,' Anya responded, matching his bantering humour. 'And,' she added, 'pheasants can only be bagged from October through to February, which, as this happens to be April, means they're out of season.'

'So you swerved.' He arched a brow. 'Because heaven forbid you should break the rules.'

Anya sighed. 'No, I swerved because I was busy thinking and it was instinctive.' A thought struck. 'Do you suppose the car's still driveable?' she asked, gazing at him in sudden horror.

Garson Deverill set off around the Volkswagen, first bending to examine the battered bodywork with long, exploratory fingers, then peering to inspect the under-carriage and finally taking a look at the engine. 'It'll be fine,' he assured her. 'Nothing mechanical's been damaged.'

'Thank heavens,' Anya said, with feeling.

He fixed her with steady blue eyes. 'And thank heavens there was no one coming in the opposite direction.'

'Like you, for instance?'

Garson Deverill glanced across at his car. 'I guess.'

Anya followed his gaze. The Maserati was a beautiful piece of machinery, the kind of vehicle which had men salivating with desire. And she had no doubt that, with his quick mind and capable actions, its driver would handle it expertly.

'I'm sure you'd have swung clear,' she said, 'but if not your insurance company would've covered the cost of any repairs.'

'They would,' he agreed, 'though the money wouldn't have bothered me. It would've been the time I'd have been forced to spend arranging everything which would've been bloody annoying.'

Anya frowned. Whilst the scenario was thankfully theoretical, she begrudged his dismissal of the financial aspect. It was a well-documented fact that many people,

herself amongst them, were having a hard time just now.
So why wasn't he similarly blighted? How come he didn't
lie awake at nights agonising over how to make ends
meet? It seemed an affront and unfair.

'Money might not bother you,' she said, 'but I have
to pay the first hundred pounds of damage on my policy,
which means—' her stomach plunged as the realisation
hit '—bang goes the microwave oven which I've been
saving up to buy.'

'So the refinements to your dream kitchen are going
to have to wait a while. That's a shame,' Garson Deverill
observed.

Opening the car door, Anya knelt on the driver's seat
and stretched over to the luggage pit in the rear. Whilst
his remark had been sympathetic, it had also insinuated
that, no matter what she had said, her financial state
could not be too dire, she mused as she began refur-
bishing the flower arrangements—which was due to her
appearance this morning. Yet, whilst admittedly her rig-
out did impart a certain affluence and a certain style,
both her blouse and trousers were around six years old
and kept strictly for important occasions. As for adding
'refinements' to her 'dream kitchen'—if only he knew
the reality!

But how did he square her ramshackle go-cart of a
car with the image she projected? she wondered. Anya
fixed the final reed. He probably believed she was pre-
tentiously and cutely slumming it.

She backed out of the car, straightened up and turned.

'The shirt collar's bent,' Garson Deverill told her. 'If
you lift up your hair, I'll fix it for you.'

Sliding her hands beneath the heavy russet fall, Anya
obeyed and he reached out to make the adjustment. As
he raised the collar and tugged at the points, his fingers
brushed against her throat. Aware of the touch, he

looked down at her and, as their eyes met and held, she became aware of a tension. A sexual tension.

'Y'know,' he said, 'you are one of the few women who should wear leather trousers.'

Anya tilted a brow. With his one-sided grin, Garson Deverill was an attractive man—the most attractive man she had met in ages—and his compliment made her feel desirable and carefree and flirtatious.

'You and your silver tongue,' she said. 'It's painful.'

He laughed. 'Sorry, but I speak the truth. Honest Injun.'

'You're trying to charm me,' Anya said, her eyes sparkling.

His hands still held the collar, but she wanted them to remain. Although she recognised that it was madness, she suddenly wanted him to thread his fingers into the thickness of her hair, draw her close and kiss her.

'Is it working?' Garson Deverill enquired. 'Have you forgiven me for splashing you?'

'Well—' She stopped in a deliberately provocative pause. 'Yes.'

'Which means my life can begin again,' he declared, grinning, then his expression sobered. 'You haven't told me your name.'

'Anya Prescott.'

His hands fell abruptly from the collar and he stood back. 'Prescott?' Garson Deverill repeated.

His double-checking could have been due to him not catching the word, yet a sharpness in his inflexion made it sound as though he had recognised her name. That it had significance. When she nodded, his gaze travelled over her, going from her russet-brown head, over her face with its high cheekbones and slightly too large mouth, to her breasts, her waist, slim hips, and finally descending down the length of her legs to her black ankle-

booted feet. He might not be touching her with his long
fingers as he had touched the Volkswagen, yet it was the
same kind of detailed and intense examination.

Anya shifted uneasily. Because she was pretty and had
a slim figure, men often demonstrated an annoying
tendency to undress her with their eyes, but Garson
Deverill seemed to be looking inside her—which was
worse. Much worse. And he was not admiring. A
moment ago his attitude has been friendly, interested,
but now she sensed something wary and almost hostile
in his gaze, as though his feelings had been redefined
and now he disapproved of her.

'I live on the outskirts of Lidden Magnor,' Anya rattled
off, in an attempt to bring an end to his discomfiting
surveillance. 'It's a village four or five miles back down
the road.'

Unblinking blue eyes met hers. 'I know,' he muttered.

Wondering whether he might explain how he knew
and why someone who was only in the country on a two-
day stopover should squeeze in an appointment in rural
Dorset, she waited—but he said nothing more. Where
was his appointment? she wondered. The local indus-
trial sites and offices were small-scale, and Garson
Deverill struck her as too high-powered an individual to
operate within the minor echelons of business.

Anya climbed into her car. 'I must go.'

'I'll direct you back onto the road,' he said, un-
smiling, and helped her to safely reverse.

'Bye,' she said through her open window.

'Goodbye,' he replied curtly.

As she drove away, Anya frowned. A hot circle seemed
to be burning between her shoulder blades and when she
looked into her rear-view mirror she saw that Garson
Deverill was standing in the road, watching her. She
moved into second, third and eventually into top gear

and, when the Volkswagen trundled around the bend which would remove her from his sight, a last glance in the mirror showed that he continued to stand with his arms folded across his chest and his piercing blue eyes trained on *her*.

CHAPTER TWO

As ANYA changed from the striped shirt and her leather trousers into a well-worn mulberry-coloured tunic and leggings, she sighed. She had assumed that yesterday's run of bad luck would be her quota for a while, yet the accident with her car this morning followed by her subsequent failure to acquire a single new outlet meant she had suffered two further calamities. Could a third be lying in wait and, if so, what form would it take? Flood, famine and a plague of mutant killer grasshoppers had yet to be sampled, she thought whimsically. And bankruptcy.

Gathering together her hair, Anya plaited it in a thick russet rope which was secured with a gold band. Think positive, she told herself. Whilst her present income would not support her and Oliver, she had sufficient cash in the bank to keep them solvent for another six months and in that time the situation was bound to improve... wasn't it?

Yes, everything would come good. After all, whilst the shopkeepers might have said that the financial climate prevented them from taking on new suppliers just now, they had also complimented her on the appeal of her products, remarked on the competitive prices, and promised to make contact the minute matters eased. But surely other shops would be more immediately receptive? They must. A list of outlets further afield had already been gleaned from the Yellow Pages and she would start on them tomorrow.

Anya frowned down at the pink and white shirt. All morning, she had felt conscious of the fact that Garson Deverill had once worn the fine poplin next to his body and now she was wearing it next to hers, of how the material had slid against his slightly tanned skin—and perhaps over curls of dark chest hair?—while today it touched her paler flesh. And the consciousness was sensual.

Anya trailed her fingertips across the shirt. Something sensual had been happening between them—until, on learning her name, his attitude had changed. Why had it changed? His reversal had been pestering in her head and now she wondered whether she might have confused weariness and hostility with simple curiosity. It was possible. Careering off the road had been traumatic, so she would have been in shock and not thinking quite straight. Which must account for that crazy desire for Garson Deverill to hold her close and kiss her.

Yet *why* should he be curious? Did her name mean something to him and, if so, what?

Dropping the shirt, Anya walked from her own small, low-ceilinged bedroom and into Oliver's even smaller one. Attempting to define the reactions of a man whom she had never met before and would never meet again was a waste of time. The shirt would be washed today and sent off tomorrow. And with its despatch the contrary Garson Deverill would be despatched from her mind.

As Anya tidied the little boy's room—straightening the dinosaur-patterned duvet, placing his much loved teddy bear on the pillow, retrieving felt-tip pens from beneath the bed—a line etched itself between her brows. Oliver had stubbornly insisted that he did not know the reason for his fight yesterday, but could it have had something to do with his father—or his lack of one?

Might the other child have been taunting him about his mysteriously absent parent?

Her heart ached. That seemed bad enough, but if it became common knowledge that she was Oliver's aunt and not his mother, as was generally believed, what taunts might the little boy be forced to face then?

Anya dropped down onto the corner of his bed. Because she had been wary of drawing too much attention to the fact that she, a single girl, had taken charge of him, when he was a baby she had allowed Oliver to believe that she was his mother. However, about a year ago, when she had felt he was old enough to understand, she had sat down with him and a photograph album and gently explained that his natural mother had been Jennie, her sister.

'But she looks just like you,' Oliver had said, peering at a photograph.

'That's because we were twins, identical twins. I loved Jennie very much and so before she died, when you were just a week old, and she asked me if I'd look after you, I said, Yes, please. Even though you had a bright red face and no hair.'

The little boy had laughed. 'And now you love me very much,' he had declared, climbing onto her knee.

Anya had hugged him. 'I love you fit to bust. But if you want to call me Aunty and tell your friends about—'

'I don't. I'm sorry my first mummy had to die,' Oliver had said solemnly, 'but you're my mummy now.'

Although she made regular references to Jennie in order to ensure that he did not forget what she had told him, the little boy seemed content with, as he called it, 'having two mummies'.

Anya plucked at the duvet. Twelve months ago, Oliver had also seemed content with her explanation of how, before he was born, his real mummy and his daddy had chosen to live apart, but last week he had suddenly started to ask questions. Where was his daddy's house? What did he do? Why didn't he ever come and see him?

She gazed blindly out of the window. Being deliberately vague, she had said that his daddy lived in London and was a musician, but had shied away from answering his third query. How could she tell a five-year-old that his sole true parent had no interest in him? She couldn't, and so she had made excuses about his father being busy. But Oliver was a bright child and she was woefully aware that he could not be fobbed off forever.

Anya frowned. Should she write to the callous and uncaring Lucan Cesari again? But if she did she knew it would be pointless. She knew he would not reply.

Switching her thoughts, Anya focused her gaze on the view from the mullioned window. She rented one of a pair of semi-detached, thatched cottages which belonged to Bob and Mavis Wright, a retired librarian and his wife, who lived in The Grange. As she looked out across an expanse of gravelled yard and past a brick barn and garages to a square Victorian house built of ochre yellow stone, she gave a rueful smile. Although, from a distance, it appeared solidly attractive, The Grange, like the cottages and the barn, was dilapidated, unmodernised and in dire need of attention. Yet it possessed such possibilities.

Her eyes swung to a weathered 'For Sale' sign. The property had been on the market for over two years, but there had been little interest and no takers.

'Thank heavens,' Anya muttered, and rose to her feet. The Wrights were presently in Australia visiting a married daughter and, as acting caretaker, it was time she made her daily check on the house.

She was halfway down the stairs when the telephone rang. Her heart leapt. Could this be one of the shop-keepers having second thoughts? She offered up a fervent prayer, but her caller turned out to be William Price, the estate agent who was handling the sale of The Grange.

'Sorry to trouble you, my pet,' said William, who, despite being in his fifties and sturdily married, had an eye for a pretty girl and a particular soft spot for Anya, 'but I was wondering if you could do me a favour? A fellow's been to view The Grange twice and now—'

'I haven't seen anyone,' she broke in, in surprise.

'No, he first came at Easter when you and Oliver were away, staying with your uncle in Yorkshire. I gather he was driving past, spotted the noticeboard and decided to take a gander. He didn't seem impressed and I wasn't surprised when we heard no more, but—what do you know?—he calls out of the blue and fixes to take another look this morning. He came while you were out.'

Anya felt a rush of trepidation. 'You did make it clear that—'

'Don't panic,' soothed William. 'I explained the entire set-up. But as the cottages are included in the sale of The Grange he'd like to see inside them, this afternoon. Unfortunately I've been landed with an unexpected client, so I was wondering if you'd warn Mr Cox that someone's coming and give the fellow a guided tour of your place for me? The Grange didn't appear to excite him second time around either, so chances are he's just going through the motions and it'll come to nothing. Will you do it?' he asked as voices sounded in the background.

'Yes, of course, but—'

'I knew you would. Thanks a lot, my pet,' the estate agent said. 'The fellow'll be with you around two-thirty. Bye.'

As the line went dead, Anya wrinkled her nose. William had been in such a rush that he had neglected to give her the viewer's name, but whoever it was she hoped they would be on time, because she had to collect Oliver from school at three. Still, a walk through her cottage would not take long, she thought wryly.

Anya went down the brick path, through the small garden where yellow and carmine wallflowers bloomed in scented profusion, and out of the front gate. As she stepped onto the footpath, she smiled. Warning her next-door neighbour to expect a visitor would not have him rushing to make everything spick and span; all it would do was make him cantankerous.

A widower in his late sixties, Bert Cox worked in The Grange's garden each morning, watched television in the afternoons and argued about politics in the village pub every evening, and he did not like his routine being disrupted by strangers who 'nosied around', as he put it.

Suddenly becoming aware of the hum of an engine behind her, Anya glanced back. A car was approaching along the leafy calmness of the lane, and, as it swung off to travel along the side of her cottage and came to a halt in The Grange's yard, she swivelled to stare. The car was a low black Maserati and the man climbing out was Garson Deverill. Her heartbeat quickened. Although she had told him she lived in Lidden Magnor she had not said where, so he must have tracked her down.

'You decided you'd prefer to have it back sooner rather than later?' Anya enquired as he walked towards her.

Her manner was amiable, yet nonchalant. She was damned if she would appear *too* pleased to see him. Even if excitement had begun shimmering through her veins, even though she suddenly found it difficult not to smile. Neither would she let him know that she had guessed he had come to apologise for his earlier curtness—and to explain. But what a change he must see in her, Anya thought regretfully, now that she had changed back into her everyday clothes.

Garson Deverill frowned. 'Pardon me?'

'Your shirt. I was intending to wash and iron it this afternoon, but if you want it now—'

'I don't.'

What a surprise, Anya thought. 'No?' she said, playing the innocent. 'So why are you here?'

'I know I'm early, but William Price said you'd show me around the cottages.'

Her jaw dropped. 'It was you who—who viewed The Grange this morning?' she faltered.

'It was,' Garson Deverill confirmed, raking back strands of dark hair which the breeze was blowing into his eyes.

Anya's mind whirled. So much for him tracking her down! So much for him coming to apologise! 'And viewing the house is the reason why you knew my name?' she enquired.

There was a split second's hesitation before he nodded. 'On my first visit, Mr Price said that you lived here with your son.'

She allowed the reference to her relationship with Oliver to ride. As people did, the estate agent had taken it for granted that they were mother and child, and she had not set him straight. She shared the truth only with close friends, or when it was essential; and always in confidence.

'I assume Mr Price also told you how the cottages are rented out, how my neighbour and I have just signed the regular one-year leases, and how we both wish to stay on after that? Stay on permanently,' Anya stressed, arrowing straight to the worry which, ever since the Wrights had put the property up for sale, had hovered like a spectre at the back of her mind.

'He did,' he replied.

She frowned. Her first impression that, on learning her name, Garson Deverill had become wary and almost hostile had been correct, because he was wary and almost hostile now. She could hear it in the clipped timbre of his voice, see it in the ice-cool light of his blue eyes. Her frown deepened. She sensed that he was not the kind of man who would affect an amiability he did not feel or let a dissatisfaction go unnoticed, yet why should *she* dissatisfy?

As Anya searched for a reason, it suddenly occurred to her that, if he bought The Grange, he could be planning to throw her and Bert out when their leases expired, feel guilty about it, and—as people sometimes did to salve their consciences—had transferred his unease into a convenient dislike for her. *She* was the obstructive tenant who wanted to remain. *She* was tarnishing his good opinion of himself. Ergo, *she* was the enemy. And if he planned to eject her and the old man from their homes it made Garson Deverill her enemy too.

Anya tugged at a silky tendril of hair which had escaped from her plait. Did the idea have any credibility or was her imagination running wild? After all, William had reckoned he was far from enamoured as a buyer.

Before she had time to decide, the protesting squawk of an unoiled door cut into her thoughts. It was her neighbour emerging from his cottage. His daily pint of milk had been left at his gate and, in shirtsleeves, red braces and slippers, he was belatedly coming to retrieve it. Anya smiled. A short, slight gentleman with white hair stuck up over his head like feathers, Bert always reminded her of an elderly pixie.

'This is Mr Deverill,' she said, taking her companion over to introduce them. 'He's interested in The Grange and he'd like to view our cottages. Would it be all right if he comes into yours now?'

Bert scowled. 'Don't have no choice, do I?' he muttered and, beckoning for them to follow, he shuffled back up the path and inside.

The cottage door was low and Garson Deverill needed to bend his head to get through it.

'You're a big bugger,' the old man commented sourly as he straightened.

'So I've been told,' he replied, unruffled, and smiled.

Whether it was the small dimensions of the room or because they were standing in a confined space between an old-fashioned mahogany sideboard, dining table and the newspaper-strewn settee Anya did not know, but Garson Deverill seemed very tall, very broad of shoulder, an imposing male presence. She eyed him warily from beneath her lashes. If he did constitute an enemy, he would not be one she could afford to ignore.

'Come from London?' demanded Bert, speaking over the sound of the television which was babbling away in the corner and which, on principle, he refused to switch off.

'I have an apartment there,' Garson Deverill told him.

The old man sniffed. 'We get a lot of outsiders trying to muscle in and grab themselves a spot of country air—don't we, Anya?'

'Some,' she agreed, wryly thinking how his attitude towards her had also altered.

When she had first arrived Bert had dismissed her as an outsider too, but, as she had offered to shop, brought round jars of home-made jam, had invited him in for the occasional meal, his scorn had been forgotten and now she and Oliver were affectionately regarded as 'us' against 'them'.

'Downstairs, upstairs, poke your nose in,' Bert said belligerently. 'Anya, you accompany him,' he ordered.

She nodded, and indicated the staircase.

'In addition to being an outsider and a peeping Tom, there's a possibility that I could possess kleptomaniacal tendencies and be tempted to stuff my pockets with whatever happens to be lying around?' Garson Deverill said, in a laconic enquiry, as they reached the landing.

Anya shone him an on-off smile. 'You can never be too careful,' she said.

Acting as guide, she conducted her charge around the house and although their tour did not take long she saw that no detail escaped him. As with his earlier examination of the damaged Volkswagen—and of her—he was intent and keen-eyed.

'I notice you're interested in the horses,' he said to Bert, when they returned to the living room. He indicated a form book which lay on the table. 'Do you get to race meetings much?'

'Not as often as I'd like,' the old man replied. 'I don't have my own transport and fixing a lift is difficult. You're done now?'

Garson Deverill nodded. 'I am. Thank you for allowing me to look round at such short notice, sir. I'm grateful,' he said, and grinned.

His host struggled to his feet. 'No trouble,' he replied, with sudden magnanimity.

As they shook hands, Anya looked on in astonishment. Admittedly Garson Deverill's grin had been beguiling, but Bert wasn't beguiled, was he? He couldn't be. He knew the threat which a new owner of The Grange could pose. He knew that in twelve months' time his home might be in jeopardy. Yet when the younger man had called him sir he had beamed and now his hand-shake was amiable.

Goodbyes were said and she led the way back towards her own house in silence. When Anya reached the white-painted garden gate, she stopped.

'Rents may be a useful income,' she said, 'but if you're thinking of doing up the cottages and increasing the rents it'd cost a mint and wouldn't make economic sense. It'd be years before you broke even.'

'True,' Garson Deverill replied, 'though I could always sell them.'

Anya frowned. Perhaps she had been naïve, but it had never occurred to her that a buyer might wish to break up the estate.

'Well, yes, you could,' she acknowledged. 'Though the cottages have always belonged to The Grange and to split them off would be a sad break in tradition. At least, I believe so, even if you think otherwise,' she said tightly, and marched off ahead of him up the path.

On following her through the low door of her home, Garson Deverill straightened up and looked around. 'I don't believe it,' he said.

Although the two cottages were mirror images in size and shape, Anya's was twice as light as the one next door, twice as bright and gave the impression of being twice as spacious—thanks to her home-making skills and long hours of hard work. The uneven walls were freshly whitewashed, colourful Indian cotton curtains hung at the small-paned windows, the artfully contrived placing of bright cross-stitched samplers added zest to a dark corner. She had stripped and varnished the floorboards, and covered them with seagrass matting. And, whilst there was adequate cheap pine furniture, there was not too much. Besides, she could not afford any more.

'It's all cosmetic,' Anya informed him. 'As with Mr Cox's house, there's woodworm in the beams, the plumbing is antique and the thatch leaks in heavy rain.'

'Even so, I'm impressed.'

Whilst it was irritating to find herself responding to the praise of a man who seemed critical towards her, Anya could not prevent a glow of pleasure. 'Thank you,' she replied, 'though everything's been done on a shoestring.'

'Have you studied interior decorating?' Garson Deverill enquired.

'No, as a matter of fact I studied French. I have a degree.'

His brows soared in blatant surprise. 'You went to university?'

'You didn't think my IQ stretched that far?' Anya asked, with a thin smile.

'I have no doubt you're as smart as a nail,' he replied, yet it was not a compliment. 'And how have you used your French?'

'After I graduated I worked as a translator in the Foreign Office, but—' Anya shrugged '—I got side-tracked. However, my mother was an art teacher and I've inherited her interest in design and colour and that kind of thing.'

'Your mother...was a teacher?' Garson Deverill queried.

'She died six years ago.'

'And your father?'

'He died at the same time. My parents were killed in a car crash,' Anya said shortly, and frowned. Why her visitor should be asking about her private life she did not know. Yet neither did she know why she was answering him. Walking to the rear of the cottage, she

brandished an arm. 'And this—boomlacka, boomlacka—is my dream kitchen.'

Opening off the living room was what amounted to
little more than a closet. True, it had a window which
overlooked The Grange's apple orchard, but it was only
large enough to contain a deep stone sink with a cold-
water tap, an ancient gas cooker and a rusting fridge.

Garson Deverill came to look inside. 'I made a
mistake,' he said.

'A major one,' Anya replied stingingly.

'But it's not a hanging offence,' he remarked, and
swung her a look, 'no matter how much you might wish
it was.' He surveyed the kitchen again. 'There's no space
for a microwave in here.'

'None, though I was intending to put it in the barn.
The Wrights allow me to use the barn as my workshop,'
she explained.

'So William Price said, and you don't pay them any
rent.'

Anya hesitated, wondering whether she should in-
terpret this as a threat. Was he indicating that if the barn
belonged to him he would demand payment?

'No, but no one had been inside the place for years
and before I could use it I needed to clear out the junk
of ages, brush away the cobwebs and paint the walls.
The Wrights say that by making the barn decent I've
done them a favour. I do them other favours too, like
keeping an eye on The Grange when they go away,' she
told him defensively.

'And where does a microwave come in?' he enquired.

'To dry my flowers. It would radically cut the time
and thus increase my production. Not all plants are
suitable for microwaving, but such things as roses,
chrysanths and daisies are ideal. And flat leaves, like
maple and elm and—' Anya stopped, aware of her en-

thusiasm carrying her away. 'The Wrights also let me take flowers from their garden.'

'And, as with the barn, if The Grange changes hands you'd like that arrangement to continue?'

'Yes, and Bert would like to continue as gardener. As you'll have noticed he does an excellent job. I'd be willing to pay rent for the barn, though not too much,' she said cautiously.

'And you pay very little for the cottage,' Garson Deverill remarked.

Not sure whether this was merely an observation or could be another threat, Anya tilted her chin. And was annoyed that she had to look up at him despite her five feet nine inches.

'I only should pay a little,' she declared, 'considering the condition it's in.'

'The low rent was your reason for taking it when you left your uncle's place in Yorkshire and moved down here four years ago?'

'Yes.' She stiffened. 'How do you know where I came from and when?' she enquired.

'I asked William Price. I asked him several things about you and your son. If there's a possibility of living cheek by jowl with your neighbours, finding out about them makes sense,' Garson Deverill said calmly, and indicated the narrow staircase. 'Please, after you.'

As Anya marched up the stairs, her lips thinned. No matter how sensible it might be, she objected to him asking questions about her—especially when he had yet to declare any firm interest in The Grange.

'This is the bathroom, Oliver's room and mine,' she said, pushing open doors in swift and impatient succession.

After looking into the first two rooms, Garson Deverill walked into her bedroom. Here Anya had painted the walls in a pale lemon, a colour which, with avocado-green and white, was repeated in the frilled curtains.

'Is that one of your arrangements?' he enquired, indicating a pretty basket of dried peonies on the pine dresser.

She nodded and gestured towards bowls of petals and leaves which added a fragrance to the air. 'I also made the pot-pourri.'

Garson Deverill subjected the room to his usual thorough scrutiny, then turned to her. 'Do you have a boyfriend?' he said.

Anya's hands curled into fists. Not content with the facts he had already garnered, he intended to pry further into her personal life? The nerve of the man! And he had obviously already pried enough to believe that she was a single parent and, most probably, an unmarried mother.

'I beg your pardon?' she said, the sharpness in her voice warning him to take the unspoken hint and backtrack.

His blue eyes went to the floral-quilt-covered bed before lifting to meet hers. 'Do you have a boyfriend?' Garson Deverill repeated.

Her heart kicked. Not only was the sexual implication in his look impossible to avoid, but it made her aware of the fact that she was alone with him in her bedroom. Alone with him in the house. Anya bit into the soft flesh of her lip. Perhaps it was because he had violated the privacy of the place where she dressed and undressed, where she slept, where she dreamed, but she felt alarmingly conscious of Garson Deverill as a hard-bodied and virile male, while she was soft and curvy and female.

'I'm sure you must've interrogated William Price as to whether or not I share my cottage with a live-in lover,' she said caustically.

'I did,' he agreed, looking her straight in the eye, 'and Mr Price said no.'

Anya spread furious hands on her hips. 'But you're worried I might have a stream of admirers driving up to my gate and banging car doors all hours of the day and night?' she demanded. 'I don't. Neither do I display a red light and pose in the porch at twilight, wearing a low-cut top, satin skirt slashed to the thigh and fish-net tights!'

As it had done that morning, the corner of his mouth twitched. 'Now that's a glow-inducing thought,' Garson Deverill drawled, 'though if you wore the trousers which you were wearing earlier I reckon you'd hook in far more customers. Your long legs and that tight little backside encased in black leather—mmm, made my palms itch.'

Anya glared. Her palms were itching right now—to slap his arrogant face. And yet, annoyingly, at the back of her mind there was an obscure satisfaction in knowing that, whilst he disapproved of her, she also appealed—albeit in a purely physical way.

'You have a fetish for black leather?' she enquired, her voice as frosty as shaved ice.

'That depends on who's wearing it.' His eyes fell. 'If it happens to be a lissom, firm-breasted—'

'To answer your question, there is no man in my life,' Anya declared, and swept out of the room and down the stairs.

She had to get away. First, to escape what promised to be a no-holds-barred description, but second, because this time when Garson Deverill had surveyed her it had been obvious that he was thinking about what she looked like naked—and she had found his gaze arousing. An ache had tightened her nipples into hard thimbles and a warmth had seeped into her skin.

Oh, heavens, he hadn't noticed, had he? Probably. Those deep blue eyes did not miss much. Yet to become aroused merely by a man's gaze was a new sensation. A troubling sensation. A shadow crossed her face. Even Dirk, whom she had once considered to be everything she desired on two legs, had never managed that.

'I believe you have a set of keys to The Grange,' Garson Deverill said, following her down the stairs a few moments later. 'Would you mind showing me through it?'

Anya's stomach knotted. She was desperate for him to leave, desperate to reassemble her wrecked composure, but, even more importantly, she had not wanted him to show any further interest in the property.

'You've looked at it twice already,' she protested.

'I'd like to look at it a third time,' he said firmly, and added, 'Please.'

For a split second Anya wondered if she dared claim to have mislaid the keys, but then she grabbed them up from the desk by the window. 'Let's go,' she said, and marched outside. 'If you did purchase The Grange would it be your main home or a weekend retreat?' she asked as the honey-coloured pea-gravel crunched beneath their feet.

'A weekend retreat,' Garson Deverill replied, 'though as I spend around sixty per cent of my time travelling I wouldn't be here every weekend.'

'If you travel so much, wouldn't it make more sense to choose a property which has easier access to airports?' she suggested.

'Maybe, but—' His shoulders rose and fell.

Anya unlocked the door and together they walked into the hall. With faded yellow wallpaper, dark brown paintwork and a scratched oak floor, it set the scene for the air of genteel and dated neglect which pervaded the whole house.

'What does your wife think about you buying a place down here?' she enquired.

Whilst Garson Deverill did not give the impression of being married, it was impossible to tell—and Anya felt an odd need to know.

'I don't have a wife,' he replied brusquely.

Her eyes met his in a challenging look. 'How about a live-in lover?'

'That neither.'

'Do you have a girlfriend?' Anya enquired.

A muscle clenched in his jaw. He plainly recognised that, as he had quizzed the estate agent, he could raise no objection to her quizzing him now—though he did not like it.

'There's no one special,' he said.

She shone him a sugar-sweet smile. 'Perhaps you're a confirmed bachelor?'

'If that's doublespeak for am I gay, I'm not,' Garson Deverill told her. 'I'm one hundred per cent heterosexual.'

'And macho with it,' Anya murmured, deliberately moving her eyes down him as he had moved his eyes down her—though she shied away from imagining what he might look like naked. That would be too disruptive to her nervous system. 'You must be catnip to women,' she said, her smile widening as she enjoyed her revenge.

'Being so much on the move, it's difficult to make relationships, let alone to sustain them,' he enunciated, in a voice which sounded like a snarl, and prowled across to look into a small room which Mrs Wright used as a sewing room. 'What would you do to bring The Grange up to scratch?' he enquired.

'Me?' Anya said in astonishment.

'You.'

When carrying out her caretaking duties, she had often refurbished The Grange in her head, and she knew exactly what she would do. Though she also knew that the question had been posed as a diversion because Garson Deverill was sensitive where his personal life was concerned.

'Downstairs I'd add a conservatory onto the drawing room,' she told him, 'and I'd revamp the kitchen and utility area.'

'Revamp how?'

'For a start, if the two storerooms were added onto here,' Anya said, walking into the white-tiled, 1940s era kitchenette, 'you could have a spacious eat-in kitchen.'

'With microwave oven?' Garson Deverill enquired.

She gave the ghost of a smile. 'Microwave, dish-washer, fridge, freezer and all mod cons. I'd give the master bedroom and the second one *en suite* bath-rooms,' she continued as they progressed to the first floor, 'and strip out and modernise the existing family bathroom. I'd also install central heating, double glazing and redecorate throughout.'

She cast him a sideways glance. 'However, all this would involve serious upheaval and a delay of many months before anyone could move in. And it'd cost tens of thousands of pounds, which, when added to the in-itial purchase price, wouldn't be worth it for just a weekend retreat.'

'In your opinion,' he said.

'In my opinion,' Anya had to admit. 'If you're looking for smart restaurants and sophisticated nightlife, Lidden Magnor isn't the place for you,' she continued.

'Did I say that I wanted nightlife?' Garson Deverill enquired.

'No, but you might. Oh, I forgot, and another thing—'

His blue eyes were raised heavenwards. 'Surely not.'

'You'd have to be around to oversee any renovations. The local workmen are good, but there are always on-the-spot decisions to be made.'

After visiting every room, they returned to the landing and he rested back against the bannister rail. 'Tell me something,' he said. 'Aren't you being *too* anti?'

'Anti?' Anya enquired.

'As I understand it the Wrights are keen to move and William Price would obviously be delighted to clinch a sale, so neither of them are going to thank you for emphasising the snags.'

Her colour rose. He had a point. Maybe she was thinking only of herself and yet, her renting of the cottage apart, the prospect of living cheek by jowl with Garson Deverill, even for the occasional weekend, filled her with apprehension.

'If I'm emphasising snags, I'm also stating the realities,' Anya protested. 'This morning you said how annoying it would've been if you'd had to spend time arranging for your car to be repaired, and arranging for this house to be renovated would demand vast amounts of time.'

He pushed his hands into his trouser pockets, drawing the charcoal-grey wool tight across his thighs.

'You're right,' he agreed.

'Taking on a place like this would mean endless hassle for someone who lived close by,' she hurried on, 'let alone for someone who is forever shooting off to far-flung lands.'

She wished he would not stand like that. His stance, resting back against the bannister, meant his pelvis was thrust out and left his manhood in no possible doubt.

'I guess,' he muttered.

He seemed doubtful. Her emphasis of the snags might not have helped the Wrights—a fact which was destined to weigh on her conscience, Anya thought regretfully—but might Garson Deverill now bow out? Might he leave her in peace? Please. Please.

His hands were removed from his pockets and he straightened. 'I understood that you collected your son from school,' he said.

'What? Yes. Every day. Oh, heavens, I didn't realise it was so late!' Anya exclaimed, looking at her watch in dismay. 'I should've picked him up five minutes ago.' She headed towards the stairs. 'Sorry, but Oliver'll be waiting so I must leave right now.'

Garson Deverill followed her out of the house. 'I'll run you to the school in my car,' he offered as she swiftly locked up.

'Thanks, but I can go in mine.' Anya flapped a distracted hand. 'I need my car keys.'

'I'm parked in front of you and I'll be quicker.'

'Even so—'

Striding forward, he swung open the passenger door of the Maserati. 'Get in,' he instructed.

'Do you train dogs?' Anya enquired.

Amusement flickered across his face. 'It's an idea if I should ever fall upon hard times. In, girl,' he said, and snapped long fingers.

She did not move. 'If I obey, you'll give me a pat on the head and a biscuit?'

Garson Deverill grinned. 'If you refuse, I'll give you a tap on that delicious rear end of yours,' he replied.

As there seemed a chance that he might carry out his threat, Anya climbed hastily inside. She did not want to accept a lift from him, but he *would* be quicker and, whatever her reluctance, it was Oliver who mattered.

'The school's beside the village green,' she said.

He nodded. 'I've seen it.'

'I hope Oliver's all right,' she fretted as they swung out onto the road. 'You hear of dreadful things happening to children these days if they're left alone, even in the space of a few minutes.'

'He'll be fine.'

'But he's only five, and although the village seems so safe and although I've told him he mustn't speak to strangers there's always—'

Garson Deverill placed his hand on her knee. 'Calm down,' he said.

Anya gulped in a breath. A moment ago she had been worried about the little boy, but now it was the warmth of the strong, blunt-tipped fingers she could feel though her leggings which bothered her. His touch had become the total focus of all her senses. Her nerves clamoured. Shock waves seemed to be rocketing through her body. She frowned. What power did Garson Deverill possess that he could cause such chaos within her?

'I am calm,' she declared, lying valiantly, and— alleluia—he removed his hand.

As the Maserati swept around the corner past the fifteenth-century church and up alongside the village green, Anya peered ahead. When she saw the mellow stone bulk of the infant school and, amongst a departing straggle of pupils, two little boys in navy blazers and grey shorts waiting patiently beside the railings, she gave a smile of relief.

'There's Oliver,' she said.

'On the left,' Garson Deverill muttered.

Anya shot him a surprised look. He was correct, but how did he know? Perhaps, together with all the other information that William Price had so garrulously imparted, he had told him how the child had dark curly hair, arched brows and a wide, uptilted mouth—all three a straight steal from Lucan Cesari—or, more probably, he could have spoken of how Oliver often resembled a bedraggled cherub. Right now, his tie hung askew and while one grey woollen sock was pulled up to his knee the other languished around a chubby ankle.

Whichever, Garson Deverill must have paid attention—and his grave expression as he gazed through the windscreen at the little boy said that he was paying attention again.

As the Maserati drew up and Oliver realised that she was sitting inside, his eyes grew round as saucers.

'This is Mr Deverill,' Anya explained, getting out to greet the child with her usual kiss and hug. 'He was viewing The Grange and he offered to bring me to collect you.'

Her chauffeur smiled out through the open window. 'Hello, Oliver,' he said.

Oliver grinned. ''Lo.'

'Would you mind giving his friend a lift home too?' Anya asked, for the other boy's mother was notoriously tardy. 'His house is on our way.'

'Sorry?' Garson Deverill sounded distracted, as though while he continued to smile at Oliver he had retreated into some private, complex world of his own. 'Oh. Yes, no problem.'

'Ace!' exclaimed the other little boy, who had been looking at the car in wonder, but as a Ford saloon drove up to pip its horn behind them he heaved a disgusted sigh. 'My mum's come,' he said, and stomped away.

With undisguised glee, Oliver climbed into the magnolia hide luxury of the back seat.

'Let's fasten your seat belt,' Garson Deverill said, and twisted round to draw the strap across him and snap the lock.

The child beamed.

'Have you had a good day?' Anya enquired as they set off back towards the cottage.

'Brill,' Oliver replied, his wide smile showing that the most brilliant event was taking place now. He leant forward. 'What's this car called?' he asked their chauffeur.

'A Maserati Shamal. It comes from Italy.'

'It's lovely. When I grow up, I shall have a car like this,' he declared.

'That's what I decided when I was about your age, and it happened. Whose class are you in?' Garson Deverill went on.

'Mrs Malcolm's.'

He grinned at the child through the rear-view mirror. 'Do you like her?'

'Yes. 'Cept when she makes us practise tying our laces.'

'You find it difficult?'

'No, it's easy. Easy-peasy!'

Garson Deverill chuckled. 'How about reading?' he enquired.

'That's easy too,' Oliver said. 'Well, the book we're on now is. And sums are—'

As the little boy chatted about his lessons and their chauffeur asked further questions, Anya listened in growing surprise. Although Oliver was friendly with people he knew, he tended to be shy with strangers; but not today. Today, he was talkative.

Could it be the thrill of riding in such a splendid car which had opened him up? she wondered. Or was it Garson Deverill's charm? His charm was potent. She had fallen victim to it this morning, until he had heard her name and switched it off, and later Bert and now Oliver seemed to have fallen under its spell.

'Thanks for the lift,' Anya said, a touch curtly, when they came to a stop on the gravel yard.

As she climbed out, Garson Deverill also climbed out, to unstrap the little boy, lift him from the back seat and set him on his feet.

'I'll give you another ride some time,' he told him.

Oliver jiggled on the spot in delight. 'Promise?'

'Cross my heart,' he declared, making the appropriate gesture across his grey-suited chest.

'Mummy, can I go and tell Grandad Bert how I came home in a Mas—Maserati?' the little boy asked.

Anya nodded. 'But look through the window first to make sure he's not having a nap,' she warned.

'I will,' Oliver said, and with a merry wave he skipped off towards the cottages.

'Grandad Bert?' Garson Deverill demanded.

'Mr Cox has claimed Oliver as a grandson and me as a daughter,' Anya said, and frowned at him across the roof of the car. 'You'll give Oliver another ride?'

He nodded. 'You see, I've decided to purchase The Grange.'

Her stomach muscles involuntarily tightened. 'Purchase it?' she echoed.

'Lord save us, the world will end,' Garson Deverill drawled, and lowered his long body into the driver's seat. Opening his window, he raised a hand in farewell. *'Au revoir.'*

This time, it was Anya who watched him go. She had wondered whether a third misfortune might befall her, she recalled as the low black car vanished into the distance—and now, whilst the world might not be on the point of extinction, she had an ominous feeling that it had.

CHAPTER THREE

WIELDING the toothpick with care, Anya applied dots of glue to the pressed purple pansy head and stuck it onto the design which she had sketched on the white construction paper.

'There,' she said.

She was experimenting with a new line—greetings cards—and five others had already been made and were stacked in a box.

'I'd buy it,' said Kirsten, from the other side of the table.

Anya gave a wistful smile. 'You and who else?'

'Lots of people,' her friend declared staunchly.

'But lots of people aren't going to have the opportunity, unless I can find more outlets.'

It was mid-evening and Kirsten had left her husband, Derek, watching television and keeping an ear open for their three supposedly sleeping children, and walked down the lane for a chat. A warm-hearted, well-rounded blonde in her late thirties, she had befriended Anya on her arrival in the village and, ever since, had provided much valued support. Kirsten had babysat, collected prescriptions if Oliver had been ill, sent the balding Derek along whenever strong-arm assistance with such matters as opening jammed windows had been required.

'And if I do drum up more business and I'm no longer allowed to use the barn,' Anya continued, 'I won't have the space to—'

'You're anticipating trouble,' Kirsten scolded. 'Nothing's been said about you not using it and, even if the Wrights have moved out, there's another three weeks before the sale of The Grange is completed and—who knows?—the purchaser could have second thoughts and the deal may fall through.'

Anya frowned out at the clouds which were creeping across the darkening sky. 'I don't think Garson Deverill's the type to change his mind once he's made it up,' she said.

'Garson Deverill's buying the place?' her friend asked, sitting up straight in astonishment. 'You just said the purchaser was a man from London. *The* Garson Deverill: tall, dark, handsome—and masterful?'

'Sounds accurate.'

'And there can't be two. Gee whiz!'

Anya tilted a curious head. 'Do you know him?'

'For sure! Not personally, of course, but I know who he is and you must know too,' Kirsten said eagerly. 'The newspapers often report on his business deals and last month *The Sunday Times* magazine featured him in an article about young tycoons.'

'I didn't see it and I don't buy a regular paper. Trying to save the pennies,' she explained.

'Well, Garson Deverill runs an international group of companies which manufacture oil-rig equipment. According to the article, he started off as an apprentice with a small firm in that line and when the owner retired he took over. He was only twenty-four, but within a few years he'd bounced up orders and the firm had expanded beyond all recognition. Since then, he's bought out several other related companies and now his group provide the full range of oil-rig gear. The article reckoned that Garson Deverill has a hard head for business and is much respected in the industry.'

'Bully for him,' Anya muttered, thinking that her impression of the man as someone who was both high-powered and successful had been correct.

'He's a handsome dog,' Kirsten continued, and gave a dreamy sigh. 'You must've thought so when you met him?'

She nodded, recalling their meeting of a month ago, a meeting which she had replayed over and over again in her head. Anya glued a yellow pansy onto the card. The good-looking Mr Deverill had packed an unforgettable sexual punch. A punch which had left her feeling . . . restless.

'I'm surprised a man like that should be single and unattached,' she remarked.

'He may be single now, but he has been married,' said the older woman, who was an ardent reader of gossip columns. 'You know Isobel Dewing, the television presenter? She started out on children's programmes and currently hosts her own what's-happening-around-town show. Smooth, swinging ash-blonde hair, willowy figure, the sweetest smile. Derek reckons she's the last word in sophistication.'

Although she did not own a television and only watched at other people's houses, Anya recalled a *soignée* blonde in a scarlet suit, with a black and white chequered shawl tossed dramatically over one shoulder. If she ever attempted a style like that, the shawl would resemble a dishrag within minutes, she thought wryly.

'I know who you mean,' she said. 'Garson Deverill was married to her?'

'Yes, they were regarded as a golden couple until they broke up—oh, three or four years ago. Apparently he prefers to keep a low profile where his private life is concerned, so there wasn't much about either their marriage or their divorce in the papers, but the split was reckoned to be due to a clash in careers.'

Anya recollected the brusqueness of his tone when he had said he did not have a wife and his remark about it being difficult to sustain relationships. 'He travels excessively, so perhaps Isobel Dewing got fed up with being left on her own so much and walked out,' she suggested, thinking that, in retrospect, his tone had hinted at a lingering hurt.

'Possible.' Kirsten frowned. 'I wonder why Garson Deverill should be interested in The Grange, when he can obviously afford something much grander, in excellent condition and in a far more up-market area?'

'It doesn't make sense to me either. And yet—' She stopped short.

'And yet what?' her friend prompted.

Anya shook her head. 'Nothing.'

She had been going to say she had a feeling that Garson Deverill's decision to buy the house might be connected with her and Oliver in some way, but the idea was ridiculous. Although he had asked a number of extraordinarily intrusive questions, he had never set eyes on them before coming to Lidden Magnor, so how could they be an influence?

Anya added fern fronds to the pansy heads and covered the design with self-adhesive film. Ridiculous or not, the idea had nagged, as persistent as a toothache, for the past four weeks—and it continued to nag now.

'Time alone will reveal his reasons,' Kirsten declared chirpily, 'and talking of time, Derek'll be expecting his supper so I'd better go.' As she rose to her feet, she grinned. 'Is God's gift to women still paying court?'

At this reference to Roger Adlam, Anya gave a groan. 'Unfortunately, yes. I've refused all his invitations out, yet now he's started to appear out of the blue with perhaps a gift of cheese, or cream, or just to chat. So he says.'

'Roger still insists that you fancy him?'

'He does, which, translated, means that with his previous dalliance having hit the skids he remains in search of a bedmate.' She wrinkled her nose. 'Each time Roger appears he tries to make me change my mind about a date and each time he assumes that I will change it—once I come to my senses and realise what a chance he's offering me!'

'He might be smug, but Roger is good-looking in a raw-boned sort of way,' Kirsten reflected.

Anya shot her a look of horror. 'You're not suggesting I should go out with him?'

'Well, you haven't dated anyone since Dirk and it's two years since he left the district. This may be antifeminist, but if it sends the sisters up the wall too bad,' her friend went on. 'When men and women were created it was with one intention—for them to link up in pairs. You were twenty-eight last birthday, which means it's high time you linked up with someone,' she pronounced, and, with that as her parting shot, she left.

As Anya put the completed card into the box and tidied her equipment away, her face clouded. Dirk Benson had been the local veterinary surgeon. They had met at a village fête and were mutually attracted. Personable, good fun and caring, the young man had seemed the ideal partner—until it had become apparent that his caring did not extend as far as Oliver.

Roger did not care for the little boy either, she mused. Indeed, the fact that she came with a child was doubtless why it had taken him so long to make advances. She frowned. The farmer's pursuit was becoming too much. A couple of days ago he had crept up behind her when she had been in the garden at The Grange and, if she had not spotted his shadow with outstretched arms, would have made a grab.

Anya's thoughts veered. The Grange. When they had moved out, the Wrights had given her a spare set of keys and asked if she would open the windows each day. 'Want to keep the place aired,' Mr Wright had bluffly declared, though she suspected that his real motive was to try and clear a persistent damp smell which, since the house had been emptied, was more noticeable than ever. But although she had opened the windows this morning she had neglected to close them.

'Damn and blast,' Anya muttered. She did not like leaving Oliver alone in the cottage for however short a time, but rain was forecast, which meant the windows must be fastened; so she would need to ask Bert to baby-sit briefly. She inspected her watch. It was another half an hour before he would make his nightly trek to the village inn, so there was ample time.

Going upstairs, Anya first checked that the little boy was sound asleep. She smiled. His thumb had fallen out of his mouth and his dark lashes were fanned on his petal-smooth cheeks. As she gazed down at him, a lump formed in her throat. She loved him so much. On the day Jennie had died, she had made a solemn vow that she would do everything in her power to protect her sister's child, provide stability for him and ensure that he was happy; and she had been successful. So far.

'Sweet dreams, babycakes,' she whispered, bending to tenderly kiss his brow.

Bert was summoned and came round, with good grace. Assuring him that she would not be long, Anya set off across the yard. As she let herself into The Grange, she hesitated. It was almost dark and the Wrights had switched off the electricity supply, so should she go back for a torch? No, a melon-sized moon, albeit intermittently masked by clouds, would provide sufficient light to see.

She shut the ground-floor windows and went upstairs, dealing first with the front bedrooms and then walking through to the back. As she secured a bolt on the final window, Anya tilted her head. She had heard a creak, like the sound of a footfall on one of the loose floor-boards in the hall. The front door stood ajar, so Roger must have been heading to her cottage on yet another surprise visit, realised she was in here, and recognised a chance to sneak up again. Her temper sparked. She objected to being ambushed.

Tucking her plaid shirt tighter into the waistband of her jeans, Anya ran down the stairs in her soft-soled shoes. The hall was empty. A cloud had covered the moon and she peered back and forth through the dark. Where was her pursuer? Another creak, this time from the drawing room, spun her around.

'Right, buster,' she muttered, 'we are going to end this here and now!'

On swiftly striding legs, Anya hurtled in through the drawing-room door to walk—slap bang!—into a tall, shadowy figure who had been coming out. She gasped and would have stumbled if two large hands had not clasped her waist and held her upright. Anya reared back, stiff as a board. She did not want the young farmer to touch her, whatever the reason. She did not want to be held. But he had refused to take no for an answer when she had turned down his invitations, so suppose he proved to be obstructive now? He was far stronger than she.

'I've had enough, Roger,' Anya warned, and raised an impetuous arm. She was a pacifist by nature, but if he attempted to kiss her she would hit him.

'No, you don't,' her would-be victim said, out of the gloom, and, grasping her wrist with insolent ease, he drew it down.

Tugging like a fiend, Anya attempted to wrench free. She would have thumped him with her other hand if he had not anticipated her intention and captured that wrist too.

'Let me go!' she demanded, squirming and pulling.

'And be punched black and blue. And hacked on the shins?' he added, avoiding her foot when she made to kick him. 'What do you think I am, a masochist?'

Anya's struggles ceased. She had recognised the voice and it did not belong to her admirer. Quite the contrary. Her breasts heaving from their fight, she gulped in a breath. 'Mr—Mr Deverill,' she stammered.

'I didn't mean to startle you, but this is my house and you're the intruder, not me,' he said, and he released her.

As the clouds cleared and a silvery light lit the room, Anya gazed up at the man who had so effortlessly hand-cuffed her. Their wrestling match might have lasted only seconds and taken place in the murky shadows of the doorway, yet how she could have confused him with the farmer she did not know. Garson Deverill was taller, broader and, wearing a pearl-grey suit which could well be bespoke Savile Row, far better dressed.

'This is *your* house?' she protested.

For a moment, he seemed intrigued by the im-passioned rise and fall of her breasts. 'I had my solici-tors push the purchase through early, in order to fit in with my movements.' In restraining her, his tie had become straggled over his shoulder in a navy silk pennant and he tucked it back inside his jacket. 'What are you doing here?' he enquired.

'The Wrights asked me to open windows and I was closing them.' Anya hesitated, wondering if he might once again accuse her of being anti about the house. 'I think there could be some wet rot, though I'm not sure.'

'There is. The surveyor mentioned it in his report. Who's Roger?'

She rubbed at her wrists. Although he had not hurt her his grip had been strong, and she could feel the imprint of his fingers burning like a brand on her flesh.

'A local farmer. He ... likes me.'

Garson Deverill's eyes narrowed. 'And you enticed the guy in here to play games in the dark?'

Anya frowned. His pronunciation of 'enticed' had been pinched with disapproval, but why should he jump to such a conclusion? What made him so suspicious and immediately think the worst about her?

'Of course not,' she replied.

He misread her frown. 'You don't seem too sure.'

'I'm positive!' She tossed back her plait. 'I told you there was no man in my life.'

'But you never said that you didn't want one,' Garson Deverill observed coolly. 'Does Roger run his own farm?'

Anya hesitated, wondering where this was leading. 'Yes, he owns the dairy farm along the road.'

'So he's a good catch.'

Her spine stiffened into a ramrod. Now she knew exactly where Garson Deverill had been leading—to the insinuation that she was a gold-digger.

'And I'm supposed to be attempting to entice him and entrap him?' Anya enquired, her eyes spitting indignant darts through the shadows.

'Hard-up girl pursues moneyed man is hardly a unique notion,' he replied.

'It's an insulting one!' she flared. 'And if I was pursuing Roger I'd try to hit him?'

Garson Deverill moved his shoulders. 'You could be playing hard to get.'

'You *are* talking utter drivel!' she retorted.

'So you didn't leave the front door open as an invitation and you aren't floating around with your shirt provocatively unbuttoned in order to—?'

'Unbuttoned?' Anya protested, and glanced down. To her horror, she saw that the top three buttons were open, exposing the honey-skinned fullness of her breasts in her white lace bra which, although it dipped low anyway, now seemed brazenly skimpy. No wonder he had been fascinated by her heavy breathing!

'They must have come undone when you *manhandled* me,' she declared, in a blistering accusation.

He ignored the charge. 'You're saying it wasn't your aim to excite this Roger?' he enquired.

'I am!' Anya snapped, fastening the buttons with hasty fingers.

Garson Deverill looked at her through the shadows. 'But you've excited me.'

His words made something jolt inside her. Jolt hard. Yet did he mean what he said . . . or could he be making a bizarre joke? Over the last few minutes he had come at her with all manner of unexpected insinuations and declarations which she had gamely answered, but now Anya was at a loss. Her chin lifted. She would not be fooled.

'I very much doubt that,' she said.

He took a step towards her. 'You want proof?'

The oxygen seemed to be sucked from the air and it became difficult to breathe. He was standing so close that she could smell the faint fragrance of his cologne and feel the heat coming from his body.

'No, thank you,' Anya said quickly.

'"No, thank you,"' Garson Deverill repeated in the same prim tone and, placing his hands on her shoulders, he bent his head and brushed his lips against hers.

It was not a kiss, just a teasing, tantalising gesture, yet it made the world reel. When he drew away, Anya did not move. She *could* not move. Her feet seemed to be rooted to the spot and her legs had turned to rubber.

'Mr Deverill,' she protested, hopelessly, helplessly.

'Garson,' he said, and his head bent again.

As his mouth covered hers, a fluttering spasm went through her. This time he was kissing her and as his tongue teased her mouth her lips parted and the hands which she had spread against his chest clutched at the lapels of his jacket. The kiss deepened, and Anya clutched tighter, glorying in the pressure of his mouth, the moist caress of his tongue, the clean, fresh taste of him. She strained closer, her breasts against his chest, her hips meeting his hips.

His mouth slowly lifted from hers. 'Convinced?' he murmured.

Like someone struck by lightning, Anya leapt back. 'I wasn't... I didn't intend to... I mean I never...' she jabbered, caught up in a bewildering mixture of intoxication and embarrassment. What had she been doing? Was she losing her sanity? Why on earth had she let Garson Deverill—a man who disapproved of her, a man who tossed out insults, a man who might be an enemy— kiss her? A breath was gulped down. 'I just—' Anya started again.

'Wanted to check that I wasn't lying?'

'No!'

He arched a dark brow. 'But you can attest to my virility?'

Remembering the unmistakable thrust of his body, Anya flushed crimson. 'Um...yes, yes,' she said jerkily, and frowned.

She had still to find a reason for her own foolish actions, yet perhaps the more pertinent question was—what had *he* been doing? A queasiness settled at the base of her stomach. With his kiss, he must have been testing her to see if she was wanton and cheap, the kind of woman who would entice. And she had appeared to give him the answer—only it was the wrong answer!

'You seem to be...affected too,' Garson Deverill remarked.

Anya stood motionless. Although his eyes had dipped, she did not need to look down to know that her nipples had tightened in a flagrant advertisement of her desire. Her face burned. Following the best tradition of male heart-throbs, he did not give a damn about his own arousal, whereas she felt exposed, humiliated and grievously betrayed.

'It's a long time since I've been kissed—so meaningfully,' she said, for a month ago she had stopped Roger's kiss almost as soon as it had started. She took several hasty steps of retreat into the hall. 'Must go,' Anya ploughed on. 'Bert's babysitting, but it's his time for going to the pub.'

'I'm leaving as well,' Garson Deverill said, and accompanied her out of the house.

When she had locked up, she held out the keys. 'These belong to you.'

'Thanks, but I don't need them. Perhaps you'd keep them, in case I should lock myself out some time?' he said.

Anya hesitated. Whatever she felt about him, and whatever he felt about her, they were going to be neighbours. His request demonstrated an acceptance of the situation, so she must accept it too, and co-operate.

'Certainly,' she agreed. 'Garson,' she added.

'Thank you, Anya,' he said, bowing his head in dry formality.

'How do you come to be here?' she asked as they walked across the gravel.

The frantic thump-thump of her heart was quietening and her blood, which had been chasing through her veins at top speed, had slowed. Now she desperately wanted to obliterate the memory of his kiss—and her foolishness—and the best way seemed to be to conduct a commonplace conversation.

'I was driving past on my way to my hotel and saw that the front door was open,' he explained. 'It looked as if there could be intruders, so I decided to check. Next thing I know we collide in the dark and you're attempting to beat the hell out of me.'

Anya gave a strained smile. She had no wish to relive their collision. 'Are you staying somewhere near?' she enquired.

'Two nights at The King's Head,' Garson replied, referring to Bert's destination and Lidden Magnor's single hostelry, a timbered black and white inn which overlooked the village green. 'Tomorrow, Saturday, I have a free day before I leave for the States on Sunday, so I thought I'd take another look at my acquisition.' He drew a tired hand down his face. 'I drove here straight from the airport.'

'Where have you come from this time?'

'Tokyo.'

'Another lengthy drive at the end of another long flight,' Anya observed.

'Too long,' he said. 'All I want to do now is collapse into a chair, have a quiet cup of coffee and go to bed.'

'I could make you a coffee,' she suggested. 'I was going to have one myself.'

Garson cast her a sideways glance. 'You're trying to humour me.'

'You guessed,' Anya replied lightly. Whilst she remained alarmingly unsure of the man—what he might do, what he might say—she would be ill-advised to be too antagonistic when, as the owner of the cottages, he controlled her destiny. Instead it would be to her advantage to try and turn him into a friend. She shone him a smile. 'I can also offer a piece of flapjack.'

'Temptress,' he said.

'Home-made flapjack.'

He spread out his hands in a gesture of surrender. 'How can I refuse?'

As they walked alongside her Volkswagen, Garson suddenly stopped to look down. On the hammered wing and beside the two dents, Anya had painted the words 'ouch!', 'pow!' and 'zap!'.

He gave a throaty chuckle. 'I like the artwork,' he said. 'Is it temporary?'

She shook her head. 'As the driving's OK, I decided that buying a microwave had priority over repairing the bumps. Though I'm not sure whether buying a microwave was the right decision,' she continued as they set off again. 'I bought it to increase my production, but for that to pay off I need to increase my trade—and it's not happening. Not by much. In the past month, only one additional shop has agreed to take—'

Anya broke off mid-sentence. Why was she telling him this? She did not usually spill out her worries with such abandon, let alone to someone who had clearly placed her on his personal blacklist. 'I'm boring you,' she said.

'Not at all.' Garson shot her a quick glance. 'I run my own company—'

'Which manufactures oil-rig equipment, I know,' Anya cut in.

She received a second look, a guarded one. 'How do you know?' he enquired.

'A girlfriend told me earlier this evening.'

'I see. Anyway,' he continued, 'as someone who's built up their own business I'm always interested when I meet anyone trying to do the same. But trade's slow?'

Anya gave a grim smile. 'Snail's pace,' she said, and explained.

Her recital ended when they entered the cottage and Bert saw who was with her. Pleased to meet Garson Deverill again, the old man jumped up to chat—until a glance at the clock showed that he was due at The King's Head.

When Bert had departed, Anya ushered her visitor towards the green and white striped sofa and opened the glass doors on the wood-burning stove. Although it was May, the evenings could be cool.

'How long have you been marketing your handicrafts?' Garson enquired as he sat down, stretching out his long legs.

'Since Oliver started school after Christmas. I wanted to be with him for his first five years, to give him a good start in life,' she said.

'You were young to forfeit your career and stay home,' he remarked. 'Didn't you find it restricting, boring?'

'Both, at times,' Anya admitted, 'and I'm glad to be out in the world again and widening my horizons. But I taught myself how to cook and sew, and—well, I wasn't too interested in me.'

'What interested you was the nuts and bolts of being a good mother,' Garson muttered, as if talking to himself. He shot her a sharp look. 'You were fortunate to be able to afford the luxury of staying at home.'

'Very, though it was only the money I'd inherited from my parents which made it possible.'

He digested this information in silence. 'Could I have a look at your handicrafts?' he asked.

Anya had been about to make the coffee, but instead she opened the box of cards and showed him a couple of garlands.

'They're good. Well made and most attractive,' Garson said.

'Thanks,' she replied, and sat at the other end of the small three-seater sofa. She could have dropped down on one of the bean bags she had made, but the thought of sitting at his feet did not appeal. Her guest might be affable right now, yet he could easily switch to the attack and if that happened she would prefer to be on his level. 'When Oliver was a baby, earning a living seemed a long way in the future and I didn't think about it in too much depth,' Anya confessed. 'I guess I'm one of nature's optimists because I always believed that something would turn up. Then, when I had the idea of selling handicrafts—'

'Why did you?' he interrupted.

'I'd made myself a dried-flower arrangement which a friend, Kirsten, admired. So I made one for her which someone else admired, and almost overnight there were orders coming in from miles around. Then I branched out into other dried-flower items and they proved popular too. Because success had just *happened*, I thought that once I started up professionally everything would streak off—' she sighed '—but I was mistaken.'

'Establishing any kind of business takes time,' Garson said.

'I'm beginning to realise that, only I don't have too much time. But selling handicrafts is ideal because it allows me to fit my working hours around Oliver and I don't want him to be a latchkey child. If the handicrafts fail, what do I do?' Anya demanded, her anxieties suddenly mounting and gathering pace. 'There's not much call for French interpreters in Dorset.'

'You have an area of excellence and you'll win through,' he said, and, reaching out, he covered her hand with his.

His touch was comforting and Anya felt a temptation to move closer and lay her head on his shoulder. It looked a strong, capable shoulder and, just for a moment, she wanted to depend on someone else instead of always having to depend on herself.

Abruptly, and as though he had only just realised the intimacy of his gesture, Garson took his hand away. 'Coffee,' he reminded her.

Anya leapt to her feet. 'Coming up,' she said, and sped into the kitchen.

When she returned carrying a tray which held two steaming mugs and a plate of flapjack, her guest had removed his jacket and was sitting with a long arm resting along the back of the sofa. Garson Deverill was a man of physical poise, she reflected. Not only did he reach out and *touch*—even if he sometimes regretted it—but now he exuded an ease with his surroundings and looked at home. He also looked drained, Anya thought as she set the tray down on a low table in front of the sofa.

'How long will you be in America?' she enquired, when she had performed her duties as hostess.

'Three weeks, and it's a whistle-stop tour,' Garson replied, and, counting off cities and states on his fingers, he proceeded to outline his schedule.

'Sounds horrific,' Anya remarked.

'At times I wonder why I push myself so hard,' he said wryly, and took a bite of flapjack. 'This is delicious.'

She smiled and sipped her coffee. In addition to wanting to humour her new landlord, she had also intended to ask him some questions, yet now she hesitated. She had been going to enquire if he was agreeable to her continuing to use the barn, whether he required rent, and—the crunch—what his long-term plans for the cottages were.

Anya cast him a glance from beneath her lashes. Kirsten had scolded her for anticipating trouble so, instead of forcing the issue, perhaps she would do better to leave well alone? Perhaps she should first try to establish an easier atmosphere between them and then—

'When did you last make love?' Garson enquired.

Startled out of her reverie, Anya almost spilled her coffee. 'Are you always so outspoken?' she protested.

'I believe in coming straight to the point. Your response earlier makes me suspect that, like your last meaningful kiss, it must've been a long time ago.'

'It was—was two years back,' she stammered.

His brows lowered. 'You had an affair?'

'I had a close relationship which I believed would be permanent,' Anya retorted, refusing to be tarred with the promiscuous brush, for that was how he had made it sound.

'But things didn't turn out that way?'

'No. Dirk—' She stopped dead, her mouth tight and her expression bleak.

'Dirk hurt you,' he said.

'Dirk *devastated* me,' Anya replied bitterly, 'but it's over.' She summoned up a measure of defiance. 'So now you know why I responded like I did. I'm a little . . . sex-starved.'

Garson looked at her over the rim of his cup. 'In that case, perhaps you'd like me to play benefactor and give

you another sample of what you're missing? If I remember, I did mention bed after coffee.'

Her hazel eyes flew open wide. A pounding started
up in her head. She might have given him the wrong
impression about her being prepared to entice earlier,
but surely he hadn't regarded her invitation to coffee as
an invitation to intimacy? He couldn't believe that her
wish to 'humour' him would stretch as far as
lovemaking?

'But *I* didn't!' Anya shot back. 'I don't know what
kind of woman you think I am, but I don't sleep around.
I'm not some prize floozie! And,' she suddenly felt it
was essential to add, 'although I did respond, my response was instinctive because—' she heard herself
starting to mangle her reply '—because you took me by
surprise and I didn't know what I was doing.'

Garson gave a brief, enigmatic smile. 'You mean it
wasn't me, as me, who turned you on?'

'Not a chance,' Anya said fiercely, but she was lying.
It had been the sensual awareness of him, *his* touch, feel
and taste, which had inflamed her.

He looked at her for a moment. 'Tell me about Oliver's
father,' he said.

Anya's fingers tightened around the handle of her mug.
Why had she answered his lovemaking query with such
candour? she wondered. What had made her mention
Dirk? And why had she told him about her business
worries? A month ago, she had resented his questions,
but this evening she had been almost force-feeding the
man with information!

She took a delaying sip of coffee. Should she say that
she was not the little boy's mother, as Garson clearly
believed? But if she did she would be forced to explain
the circumstances of Oliver's birth, which would mean
revealing that her sister had once danced with a well-

known pop group and had had an affair with the lead singer.

Anya frowned. Although the truth was not sleazy if you had known Jennie the way she had, it *sounded* sleazy, and she baulked at divulging it—especially to a man who had so recently attributed sleazy intentions to her.

'There's nothing much to tell,' she said offhandedly. 'There was a romance and Oliver was the result.'

'His father didn't feel inclined to marry you?' Garson enquired.

Anya thought of how, when her twin had told Lucan Cesari she was having a baby, his response had been an instant denial of responsibility. A denial which had left Jennie feeling bemused and bereft and deserted.

'No,' she replied.

In the silence which followed, a log crackled and fell on the fire.

'The last time I was here you told me your ideas for upgrading The Grange,' Garson said, in a gymnastic change of subject. 'You mentioned redecoration and I was wondering whether you had any ideas about that too.'

Relieved that he was enabling her to abandon the quicksands of deception and step onto firmer ground, Anya smiled. 'I do.'

She talked about how she would white-gloss the woodwork, of colour schemes, even about the wallpaper which she had envisaged for various rooms.

'Could you suggest firms who might do the work?' Garson enquired. 'The major alterations as well as the decorating.'

Anya nodded. 'In delivering my flower arrangements I've visited several houses which have been having extensions built or other improvements made, so—' She broke off.

He had bent to absent-mindedly scratch at his ankle and in doing so had rucked up his trouser leg. Above the top of his sock she could see a couple of inches of smooth, tanned calf.

Garson sat back. 'So?' he prompted.

Anya blinked, aware that she had been staring as if transfixed. But to be transfixed by a glimpse of a man's leg was inane, juvenile, pathetic. She was acting like some daffy schoolgirl, not a mature and self-sufficient young woman.

'So I can recommend builders, plumbers, electricians, et cetera, all of whom work to a high standard and have a good reputation,' she rattled off.

For another quarter of an hour, they continued chatting about The Grange, until Garson stretched and tiredly yawned.

'Thanks for the coffee and for your ideas,' he said, climbing to his feet, 'but if I don't go you'll be stuck with a comatose figure stretched out on your sofa for the night.'

Anya's heart lurched. The thought of him lying there seemed inordinately engaging. Having a virile, sexy man around the place held a definite appeal. She jumped up. She must be having a brainstorm.

'I understand The King's Head is comfortable, though a little homely,' Anya said as she opened the door, 'so I'm afraid it'll be nothing like the hotels where you usually stay.'

'Thank the Lord,' Garson replied. 'I've had enough super-efficient and totally anonymous towers of marble and glass to last me a lifetime.'

As he looked at her, his eyes fell to her mouth. Anya's heartbeat quickened. Was he going to kiss her? she won-

dered, her feelings finely balanced between heady elation
and utter dismay. And, if he did, would she, could she
resist?

'Good—goodnight,' she stuttered.

'Goodnight,' Garson replied, and, ducking through
the doorway, he strode off down the path and into the
night.

As Anya finished drying the breakfast pots, she looked
out of the window. The rain which had been forecast
had fallen overnight and the sun was shining.

She checked her watch. It was nine o'clock. Garson
would be coming to take a look at The Grange this
morning, but his tiredness would mean a late start and
by the time he arrived she intended to be gone. After a
night of tossing and turning before eventually falling into
a fitful sleep, she wanted to avoid her new landlord. Her
reaction to his kiss had revealed a dangerous vulner-
ability which she preferred not to put at risk again. With
time, her erratic emotions would settle down, but until
that happened the less she saw of Garson Deverill the
better.

Going upstairs, Anya collected towels and swimming
gear. She had decided to take Oliver to Lulworth Cove.
It was rare that they had a day at the coast—days out
cost money—but he would enjoy it and a change of scene
must help calm her frayed nerves. Sunhats were added
to the holdall. She was ready. All she needed now was
to rope Oliver in from The Grange's garden where he
was playing, give him a quick wash and they would be
off.

As Anya walked past the barn and onto the carpet of
lawn, her footsteps slowed. She could hear voices.
Oliver's piping tones interspersed with an adult male
rumble. Squinting against the sunshine to the den which

the little boy had built amongst bushes at the wilder end of the garden, she caught a glimpse of a figure in a navy and white checked shirt hunkered down. Her heart sank. Oh, no, Roger must be here. She was thankfully thinking that he would not make a grab for her while the child was around, when Oliver's voice wafted across the lawn.

'I have a great-uncle—my uncle David who's married to my aunty Jane and who's gone to live in Brazil,' she heard him say, 'but most of my friends have proper uncles. Henry Collis has lots. Another one's just come to live with Henry and his mummy, and he buys him pizza and video games. And,' the little boy added, with a giggle which sounded suspiciously like a snigger, 'Henry's uncle and his mummy have their baths together!'

Anya grimaced. Henry Collis's 'uncles' were the talk of the village. Since his father had moved out last year, the child had already had three, the latest of whom, a tattooed individual who sold second-hand caravans, had moved in with the fickle Mrs Collis two months ago. Her brows knitted. Now that she remembered, it had been Henry Collis whom Oliver had fought.

The low rumble sounded beyond the bushes, then Oliver piped up again. 'Please will you be my uncle?' he appealed.

Anya leapt forward. Oliver was asking Roger to become her lover? Would that be a nightmare or what!

'It's time to leave,' she called, sprinting across the grass. 'Oliver, you need your bucket and spade, and—' As the man who had been crouched on his haunches stood erect, Anya broke off and stopped dead. 'Oh, it's you,' she said, looking at Garson Deverill with wide, startled eyes. 'I thought it was Roger. After all, it's early and—' she glanced over her shoulder '—your car's not here.'

'It was a fine morning so I walked,' he said, and came across the lawn towards her.

One night's sleep had transformed him. His weariness had disappeared and he brimmed with energy. In the casual checked shirt, close-fitting jeans and handmade tan leather boots, he looked younger, athletic and more muscular. Like a healthy panther, Anya thought, unable to ignore the graceful stride of his long legs; an inquisitive, interfering, disruptive panther!

'Where are your bucket and spade?' she asked Oliver, who was skipping happily along beside him.

'In my toy box.'

'Go and get them,' she instructed.

The little boy smiled up at Garson. 'Bye.'

'Bye,' he replied, ruffling his hair, and the child ran off towards the cottage.

'I would prefer it if you did not quiz Oliver about the relatives he may or may not have,' Anya said, in a voice as cold as the Arctic. 'His personal circumstances are none of your business.'

'I wasn't quizzing him,' Garson said. 'He brought up the subject himself.'

'Oliver did?' she protested.

He nodded, and hooked his thumbs into the slit pockets of his jeans. 'I have a proposition to make. I was wondering if you'd walk through The Grange with me and spell out all your improvement ideas in detail. Then, when we've agreed on what's to be done, whether you'd be willing to contact the necessary firms on my behalf and oversee the work.'

Anya gave a surprised laugh. 'You'd trust me to organise everything?'

'Shouldn't I?' Garson enquired, turning the question back onto her.

'Yes, I could do it, but—' she hesitated '—I doubt my improvement ideas will go far enough.'

'Why not?'

'They're pretty conservative and, well, you could be thinking of installing a bar, or Jacuzzis, or adding a swimming pool.'

'And I'd want chandeliers and gold taps and mirrored ceilings all over the place?' Garson said.

His shirt neck was unbuttoned and as she faced him her gaze went to the open V. She had wondered if he had a hairy chest, Anya remembered, and he did. His skin was covered with a dark cloud of curling hair. Coarse, lustrous hair.

'Er . . . possibly,' she said, her cheeks pinkening as she realised he was waiting for an answer.

Garson shook his head. 'Perish the thought. I may drive a Maserati, but I'm a down-to-earth kind of a guy.'

'You are?' she said doubtfully.

'I am. Naturally I'll pay you a wage,' he went on, and named a weekly sum. 'How does that sound?'

'It sounds very generous,' Anya replied, for he was offering three times the amount which her handicrafts were currently bringing in. Her chin tilted. 'However, I can manage without your patronage.'

'Patronage?' Garson queried.

'Yesterday evening I told you how my trade is slow—'

'And you think I'm suggesting you work for me because of that?' he interrupted. 'You think I'm offering charity? Sweetheart, what I'm suggesting is that *you* cope with the endless hassle which I can well do without.'

Idiot! Anya thought. She should have known that Garson Deverill would not give her a handout. She ought to have realised he was not in the business of helping her, but was helping himself.

'My heart sings,' she said pertly.

His mouth tweaked, making her realise that, whatever his reservations about her, she could still make him smile.

'What's your answer?' he enquired.

'I'm not prepared to abandon my handicrafts,' she told him, 'so I couldn't be in attendance or at your beck and call every hour of every day.'

'I don't expect that,' Garson assured her. 'Though if there should be problems I'd need you to be here to act as troubleshooter.'

Anya frowned, assessing his proposition. 'I'll do it,' she said.

CHAPTER FOUR

ANYA closed the large book of fabric samples, heaved it to one side of the counter and dragged across another. Three alternative designs had already been chosen for the curtains in each of The Grange's four bedrooms, for the drawing room, and now she was searching for ideas for the dining room. As the room was oak-panelled, she and Garson had agreed that the curtains should be of a traditional pattern in rich oil-painting colours, so how about this gold on burnt sienna fleur-de-lys? A note was made of the reference number.

Usually she mailed samples—whether of curtain fabric, or cork flooring, or etched glass for shower panels—to Garson's secretary in London, who, in turn, either showed them to her boss or sent them express to wherever he happened to be, but this evening Garson was coming to Dorset for the weekend and so could make his decision straight away.

'I'd like to take these,' Anya said, when the shop owner, who had been out to The Grange to measure up, came to ask how she was getting along. 'I'll return them on Monday.'

'They're stylish designs,' the man remarked as he amassed the samples. 'Mr Deverill should find something to suit him.'

'I'm sure he will,' she agreed.

It was amazing how their tastes matched, Anya reflected as she drove out of the town-centre car park and onto Sherborne's winding streets. Only once had Garson objected to her choice—he had asked that she send samples of ivory-coloured bathroom tiles to replace white, and when the tiling had been done she had had to agree that the warmer tone was more attractive.

It was also amazing how smooth and trouble-free their liaison had been, which was why, now that the house alterations were nearly complete, he had asked if she would handle the installation of carpets, curtains, blinds for the conservatory et cetera.

Anya turned into a road signposted for Lidden Magnor. Over the past eight weeks there had been a shift in Garson's attitude towards her. His hostility had faded and he was amicable. However, a continuing though muted wariness indicated that her name had not been erased from his blacklist, merely moved lower down.

But why had she been blacklisted in the first place? The theory about him intending to oust her from her cottage and feeling guilty did not convince—he had never once hinted that way—yet she had failed to find another reason. Anya shrugged. If Garson had some hang-up about her that was his problem. But what did she feel about him? She frowned out at the road ahead. Whilst she was grateful for his help in keeping the wolf from the door, at the back of her mind lurked the uneasy suspicion that *he* might be the wolf.

On his three flying visits Garson had kept his distance, Anya mused as she drove along. There had been no more 'testing' kisses. This was a relief, and yet, although he had not touched her again, to her each encounter had seemed intensely *physical*. She was forever conscious of him as six feet plus of male flesh and blood—and alarmingly appealing flesh and blood.

Still, her work at The Grange would soon be finished and they would have far less contact, she thought, comforting herself. Garson would no longer be able to impinge on her senses. Her thoughts zigzagged. And she would no longer receive his weekly wage.

Drawing down the visor, Anya cut out the glare of the sun. Luckily the influx of summer visitors into the area had boosted sales in her disappointingly static number of outlets, but in the autumn the money problem seemed destined to raise its ugly head again. Don't become neurotic, she told herself. You've survived this far and will continue to survive.

Anya took a quick look at her watch. Today, because Oliver had been invited to a birthday party straight from school, she had been on the go from nine until six. From Yeovil to Dorchester to Sherborne she had travelled, tracking down brass doorknobs, assessing wall lamps, buying hooks for the cloakroom which had replaced the old sewing room, and now she had just enough time to get home and collect him.

'Mr Deverill will call in to let us know he's arrived and see me before I go to bed?' Oliver demanded, a couple of hours later.

'That's what he said,' Anya replied, a mite wearily, for he had asked the same question several times before.

They were in the garden at The Grange. The little boy was hitting around a shiny silver balloon which he had brought back from the party while she cut flowers in preparation for a dried arrangement. It was a balmy evening. Overhead an arrow of ducks flapped their way across the sunlit sky, while in distant fields a cow gave a soporific moo.

'I can stay up until he comes?' Oliver enquired, needing yet more confirmation.

'Yes.' Garson's stated landing-time meant that he should reach Lidden Magnor around eight-thirty, which was fast approaching. 'Unless his plane's been delayed and he's very late,' Anya added as a precaution.

'If his plane was delayed, Mr Deverill would've sent us a fax,' Oliver declared with the confidence of one who knew, and like a young puppy who needed exercising all the time he launched himself back into his game.

Anya cut a long-stemmed head of hydrangea. When she had agreed to work for Garson, she had also agreed that a fax machine should be installed in her cottage to facilitate the passing of information, queries and replies between them. As a child of the technological age, Oliver had quickly learned how the machine functioned and begged to be allowed to send a message. This he had done and when her new employer had replied with the suggestion that the little boy send him regular letters or drawings a back and forth correspondence had begun.

Anya examined the petals for blemishes. She had thought that Garson's lack of time—and a lack of real interest—would soon wither the arrangement away, but it had continued. And their correspondence, allied with his visits, meant that he and Oliver now shared a surprisingly warm relationship.

Anya walked into the barn. Whilst the little boy derived much pleasure from this, she had misgivings. She did not want him to become *too* close to a man who was only a neighbour, and a disturbing unfathomable neighbour, at that. How much did she know about Garson Deverill? she brooded as she pinned the flowers to a line to dry. Very little. Whilst his work was casually referred to, he had volunteered no information about his private life.

'He's come!' Oliver shouted joyfully from outside, and when Anya went to the door she saw the Maserati purring onto the yard.

With a sense of rising anticipation, she watched as Garson climbed out of the car—a tall, now familiar figure in the usual immaculate business suit. Her skin prickled as if from a thousand tiny electric shocks. Her heartbeat quickened. Anya swallowed down a breath. To react in such a way was both pathetic and annoying, yet it happened each time they met.

As she walked forward, Garson bent to lift Oliver up into his arms. Anya frowned. The little boy was chattering away as though he couldn't get the words out fast enough, and looked so happy and so at ease.

'Mr Deverill's here for four days,' he informed her importantly as she drew closer.

Anya felt poleaxed. Derailed. Out of sync. She had been prepared for a weekend, but the news that he would be staying twice as long seemed more than she could take.

'You didn't mention it before,' she said.

'And now you'd like to chop off the protruding parts of my body?' Garson enquired.

Her cheeks flushed scarlet. Had the edge to her voice been *so* obvious?

'No—'

'I won't be forced to speak soprano?' he said drolly. 'That's a relief.'

'It's just a surprise, that's all,' she completed.

'I only decided on the spur of the moment,' Garson said, 'and I was wondering if, while I'm here, we could take a look at some furniture?'

Anya pasted on a bright smile. 'Suits me.' If she was to help with the furnishing of The Grange it would mean an extension of her wages, she realised, which made her want to cheer. Her mind tripped. But it would also mean an extension of their involvement, which did not. 'You're a big boy to carry,' she said, switching her gaze to Oliver, who had an arm slung affectionately around his hero's neck. 'Mr Deverill must be getting tired.'

'I'm exhausted,' Garson replied, and put the child down, although she knew he was only conforming to her wishes. 'Does it have to be Mr Deverill?' he enquired as he stood upright. He tugged at the knot of his tie, loosening it and drawing it down an inch or two in what struck her as an outrageously sexy gesture. 'It's very formal.'

'Perhaps, but I don't consider he should call you Garson,' she said. 'He's too young and—'

'It's too familiar?' he cut in.

'Well—yes,' Anya agreed, bewildered because he had suddenly sounded aggressive.

'I could call you Uncle Garson,' Oliver suggested hopefully.

Visualising Henry Collis's assortment of 'uncles', she shook her head. 'You're to stick with Mr Deverill. And now that he's arrived and you've seen him it's bedtime.'

Oliver's lower lip projected. 'No.'

'You've stayed up an extra hour already,' Anya said, 'and even though you don't have school in the morning—'

'I'm not going to bed!' the little boy squealed, stamping his foot in an abrupt red-faced tantrum which took her by surprise.

'Now, Oliver—' she began.

He batted furiously at her with his balloon. 'Not going!'

'Hey, stop that,' Garson instructed, and, as if a switch had been flipped, Oliver's yelling and batting ceased. 'You do what your mother tells you. Always. In any case, I'm leaving now,' he said, bending down to speak more gently to him. 'I have to check into The King's

Head and find out whether or not they can put me up for the extra days. I'll see you tomorrow. OK?'

Oliver bowed his head, scuffed his feet and gave a shamefaced smile. 'OK,' he mumbled.

'So, no more histrionics, you little horror,' Garson said, with a wink, and the child giggled.

Watching, Anya felt torn. One part of her was grateful for his intervention, but another part resented it. Oliver lived in *her* care and was *her* responsibility. Garson had no right to admonish him.

'Come along,' she said, taking hold of the small, rather grubby hand which fitted into hers like a warm field mouse. 'It's into the bath for you.'

As Oliver readjusted his grip on the string of his balloon, Garson spoke *sotto voce* into her ear.

'I'd like to come back after I've checked in and had something to eat,' he said. 'We need to talk.'

Anya nodded. His talking would be about the furnishing of The Grange.

Although Oliver chattered non-stop as she bathed him—about the party, but also about his friend, the marvellous Mr Deverill!—by the time he was tucked up in bed he had begun to yawn. His thumb went into his mouth, his teddy was cuddled, and before she had left the room he was almost asleep.

Downstairs, Anya tied the silver balloon to a chair and cleared away the remnants of birthday cake which Oliver had brought home. There had been a clown at the party. Could he have a clown at his next party? Please? the little boy had appealed. Everyone, it seemed, had clowns, or ponies to ride, or hired bouncy castles to play in.

Her face grew troubled. Whilst she had promised to 'think about it', she hoped that he would forget; if not, her budget was going to demand some serious massaging. And what happened when Oliver grew older and wanted the latest mountain bike, or a computer, or to go on school holidays with his friends? That was when the shortage of cash would really bite.

A knock on the door made a sharp intrusion into her thoughts. Garson had returned already? That was quick. But perhaps The King's Head could not take him for four days and he had come to tell her he was going to book in elsewhere? Thank goodness she did not have a spare bed, Anya thought as she crossed the room. Then she might have felt obliged to offer accommodation, but if Garson slept in the same house he would be too close for comfort. Something fluttered inside her. Much too close.

Anya tweaked at the V-neckline of her pink button-through dress, lifted her plait back from her shoulder and opened the door. Her eyes widened. It was Roger Adlam who stood beneath the porch.

'Hello, stranger,' she said, and her gaze travelled to where his pick-up truck was parked outside on the lane. 'Is Fiona with you? How's the big romance?'

Back in May, the young man's pursuit had suddenly ceased and, a week or two later, Kirsten had reported that he was seeing the daughter of a fellow farmer—a homely, apple-cheeked girl whom Anya had met at quiz nights. And Kirsten's latest bulletin was that Roger reckoned he had found true love at last, while his girlfriend was excitedly whispering to her friends about an engagement.

'The romance isn't,' he replied.

'You and Fiona have fallen out? Never mind,' Anya said soothingly, 'I'm sure you'll soon get back together again.'

Roger laughed, short and harsh. 'No way. You see, we haven't fallen out, it was yours truly—' he poked his thumb at his chest '—who walked out.'

'Why?' she protested. 'Fiona's a lovely girl.'

'Lovely, but dull,' he declared damningly, and would have pushed past her into the cottage if Anya had not stretched out her arms to clasp the wooden side posts of the porch and block his entry. The young man frowned and cleared his throat, as if deciding that a speech was necessary. 'You will forgive me,' he said, though it sounded more like a statement than a question.

'For what?' Anya asked.

'For deserting you. You must've been so hurt, but you don't need to shed any more tears because I've returned,' Roger announced, and paused as if expecting her to break into loud hosannas. When these were not forthcoming, he continued, 'You're different from the other girls around here. You have far more sparkle, far more style. Forgive me,' he said and, reaching out, he jerked her hard against him and buried his face in the hollow of her neck.

As she felt the slither of his lips, Anya's skin crawled. 'Get away from me,' she said.

Roger raised his head. 'Away?' he echoed, in astonishment.

'Away!'

He released her. 'Anya, I know—'

'You know nothing,' she said, 'and that's because you have an inflated idea of your own attraction and the hide of a rhinoceros. However, I'm about to increase your knowledge, so pay attention! I did not shed a single tear when you stopped calling because I was relieved.'

'But—'

'I said pay attention,' Anya instructed, her voice ringing out. 'Earlier in the year, although I made it abundantly clear that I was not interested in anything more than friendship, you pestered me. I have no wish to quarrel, but I'm not prepared to be pestered again. So go—go back to Fiona who loves you and who believes that you love her.'

During her tirade, Roger's fresh outdoors colour had heightened to puce. 'Yes, Anya,' he said meekly, and stepped back off the porch.

As he moved, opening up her view, she saw Garson standing on the pavement at the corner of the fence. She looked at him in surprise. His suit had been exchanged for a black short-sleeved shirt and blue jeans, and he held a duty-free carrier bag in one hand.

'I guess I did pester,' Roger confessed, drawing her gaze back to him. He seemed about to launch into an uncharacteristically humble admission of errors when he, too, caught sight of Garson. 'I'm sorry,' he said gruffly, and, with a curt nod in the older man's direction, the farmer marched out to his pick-up truck, jumped into the cab and drove away.

'Bravo,' Garson said as he came up the garden path. 'That was magnificent.'

'I assume you heard it all?' Anya asked.

'Couldn't miss it, I'm afraid. I'd gone in to have a look at The Grange and when I came round here you were in full flow. Then it seemed that if I made an exit I might interrupt the grand denunciation.' He grinned. 'Forget about me training dogs, you'd be no slouch as a lion tamer. At one point I thought you were going to go after the poor guy with a whip.'

'Poor guy nothing,' she retorted. 'In my opinion, Roger is a pompous jerk and a menace.'

'So I gathered, though judging from how he slunk away with the proverbial tail between his legs he won't dare be a menace again.' Garson raised mock-anguished brows. 'We've had a few battles, but heaven forbid that you'd ever do a demolition job like that on me.'

'You'd cope,' Anya said spikily.

'You don't think my tail would droop?'

'Never.'

There was the blue crackle of direct eye contact. 'Damn right,' Garson said. As they went indoors, he produced a magnum of Krug champagne from the duty-free bag. 'I wanted to celebrate The Grange's transformation and to thank you for making it happen,' he explained, when she looked at the bottle in surprise. 'Do you have a corkscrew?'

'Yes, but I don't have any champagne flutes. All I can offer are water tumblers.'

'They'll be fine.' A few moments later the cork came out with the statutory pop and he poured two foaming glasses. 'With my sincere appreciation for all your efforts,' he said, toasting her.

'It's been fun,' Anya replied, and took a sip, laughing when the bubbles tickled her nose. 'This is fun too. I can't remember when I last had champagne.'

'Then enjoy. You do realise that you're your own worst enemy?' Garson asked.

'How?' she asked, walking over to the desk to switch on the table lamp. The translucent apricot sky of the evening was gradually darkening and shadows were filling the room.

'You said the refurbishment would take many months, which was feasible, yet you've been so efficient, organising everything down to the last detail and dovetailing the tradesmen to eliminate waiting days, that it'll be done in not much more than two.'

Anya took another mouthful of sparkling champagne. Her efficiency had been inspired by the determination to show Garson that she was hardworking and capable, though she did not know why impressing him should matter so much.

'As the saying goes, if a job's worth doing it's worth doing well,' she replied brightly. 'Besides, I have no wish to take advantage of your generosity.'

'I appreciate that,' Garson told her. He topped up their glasses and they sat down together on the sofa. 'I owe you an apology,' he said, his tone and his expression serious. 'I accused you of enticing Roger and implied that you might be avaricious and...flighty. I got it wrong. Badly wrong. I realise that now.'

Anya smiled. The words were honey to her ears and balm to her soul. To know that she had been taken from his blacklist was sweet, and her conviction that it would be rare that he said sorry—rare that Garson made mistakes to say sorry for—made his apology all the sweeter.

'You're going to kneel at my feet and beg for absolution?' she enquired, her eyes dancing.

He chuckled. 'I'll prostrate myself full length on the floor if you so desire.'

'Yes, please,' Anya said smartly.

Garson gave a despairing groan. 'What ever possessed me to make such a dumb suggestion?'

She laughed. 'Are you trying to wriggle out of it?'

'No, though if I go down on the floor you're coming with me and then—' his blue eyes locked with hers '—I could well be tempted to possess you.'

Anya's heart started into an erratic beat. In the glow of the lamplight, Garson looked intense, a man of passion. This was not some test he was giving her. This time he meant what he said.

'You're a lovely young woman and for you to sleep alone every night is a shameful waste,' he said, his voice low and husky.

'When you're bringing up a small child, there isn't much time or opportunity for relationships,' she replied lightly, then shot him a glance. 'It's the same as if you're continually on the move.'

'Touché,' Garson murmured.

'Besides, the Dorset social scene is not exactly *knee-deep* in males prepared to saddle themselves with— Whoops!' As she had been speaking, Anya had swung a hand in emphasis. It was the hand holding her glass, which had tipped and was now dribbling champagne. She set the glass on the low table. 'With a woman plus child,' she finished.

Anya started to raise the champagne-wet fingers to her mouth, but as she did Garson put down his own glass, caught hold of her wrist and steered her fingers from her lips to his. 'Let me,' he said, and started to lick away the trickles of pale golden liquid.

She sat mute. The rasp of his tongue on her skin seemed to have robbed her of speech, of any power to protest. Though did she want to protest?

'I could become addicted to this,' Garson murmured, closing his lips to suck along the length of her index finger from its base all the way up over her knuckles to the tapered unvarnished nail.

She gazed into the deep blue of his eyes. 'Mmm,' she managed weakly, and swallowed, aware that, as when she had stared at his leg, she was being inane, juvenile and pathetic. Anya shone him a giddy smile. 'I like it too,' she declared.

After sucking each of her fingers in turn, an act which made her bones seem to melt and her head spin, Garson bore her back against the soft cushions.

'I wonder if your lips taste of champagne?' he said, and swiftly kissed her.

Anya laughed. Garson was teasing, playing, flirting with her, and she wanted to tease, play and flirt too.

'Do they?' she asked, smiling at him.

'No. I think more like—' he kissed her again '—strawberries.'

'Strawberries?' Curling an arm around his neck, Anya tugged at the thick dark hair which grew at his nape. 'Never.'

Garson gave her a third quick kiss. 'You're right,' he declared. 'Nectar.'

This time she had no chance to protest, for his mouth covered hers and he kissed her again, seriously and deeply. Anya's heart began to hammer. As when he had licked her fingers, his tongue was working a drugging kind of magic, only a different, more potent magic—a magic which was creating a hunger inside her. And when the kiss became another and another the hunger grew.

Eventually, he raised his head. 'More?' he enquired.

Anya saw that his lips were swollen and softly bruised. Presumably hers were too. 'More,' she replied.

As Garson drew her close and kissed her again, rivers of fire seemed to flow through her veins. He shifted his weight and his hand moved up between them to cover one firm, up-tilted breast. Anya's pulses raced. Her nipples had risen, taut and aching, and he was moving his fingers over her breast in slow, caressing circles which grew smaller and smaller until, in a tantalising moment, his thumb grazed across the tight point.

She drew in a breath. The thinness of her dress made it feel as though he was touching her naked breast— almost. As he fondled her again, Anya stirred restlessly. The hunger she felt was becoming a need, a fierce, compulsive need. She needed him to undress her, to press his mouth to her bare skin, to suckle her.

'I wonder if the rest of you tastes as good?' Garson said, and his eyes fell to the curve of her breasts and the jutting promise of her nipples. 'All of you.'

Anya's heart started to slam against her ribs. Her need was matched by his. She could see it in the glazed look of his eyes, feel it in the fevered heat of his body, hear it in the hoarseness of his voice. Garson wanted to make love to her and she wanted it too. So very much.

Afterwards Anya would wonder what it was that had made her draw away and would decide that although it could have been native sense—he was, in reality, not much more than an acquaintance and their relationship tended towards the uneven, to say the least—it might just as easily have been the realisation that if their love-making continued Garson would see her underwear, which, being the everyday set, meant a much washed, slightly fraying white cotton bra and panties with questionable elastic.

'The location's lousy,' she declared, smiling at him as her brain frantically devised a way of extricating herself.

Garson looked bemused. 'Location?' he echoed.

'We shouldn't be sitting on a bargain-basement sofa in a living room. We should be lying amidst satin sheets in a sumptuous four-poster bed, with me—' Anya ignored the frustration which was gnawing at her '—clad in a diaphanous negligée with something fragile made of French lace underneath.'

He frowned, but a moment later his hand left her breast to move to her shoulder where he fingered a burnished strand of russet-brown which had escaped from her plait. 'With your hair loose and streaming out in rippling waves over the pillow?'

Grateful that he was willing to follow her lead, she nodded. 'Yes. Though the champagne seems to have gone to my head, because embarking on a romance is not one of my priorities right now.'

'Nor mine,' Garson said, and, rising to his feet, he crossed over to the window. He gazed out into the darkness. 'The champagne's affected me too,' he muttered, and she knew from his retreat and the rigidity of his stance that he also had misgivings about their lovemaking.

'You wanted to talk about The Grange,' Anya said, adopting a businesslike tone. She might be at the mercy of romantic longings, but she refused to dwell on them. And if she wanted them to make love it was just a temporary glitch. 'What did you think when you went in there just now and saw the fresh paintwork and the finished conservatory? Were you pleased?'

Garson turned to face her. 'I was delighted. Everything's perfect.'

'Isn't it,' she agreed, and felt a glow of achievement. She smiled. 'I knew the house had potential, but I never dreamed it'd make such a beautiful home.'

'It's turned out far better than I imagined too. But I didn't say I wanted to talk about The Grange.' He walked back to stand in front of her. 'I don't know how to tell you this.'

'Tell me what?' His expression was grave and he seemed uncharacteristically hesitant. As Anya gazed up at him, a band tightened painfully around her chest. 'It's the cottages,' she said in a leaden voice. 'You're going to sell them.'

'No.'

'Well, now that The Grange is renovated, you want to renovate them?'

Garson lowered himself down into the other corner of the sofa. 'Yes, I do,' he said, 'but—'

'And the rents will be increased.' Anya shivered as the spectre which she had once feared and had latterly ignored rose up again in her mind's eye. Why hadn't she insisted on knowing his plans right from the start? she wondered. Why had she foolishly allowed the matter to lie?

'I'll have to leave Lidden Magnor because there's nothing else affordable which I can rent here, but I don't want to leave. I wanted to stay here for *always*,' she said, and her voice cracked. 'Still,' she went on, adopting a doughtily bright tone, 'if I have to move and start over again, so be it. I'll manage. I'll—'

'Anya, although I intend to renovate the cottages I shan't be increasing the rents,' he told her.

She looked at him in disbelief. 'You won't?'

Garson shook his head. 'No. I don't want either you or Bert to leave.'

'Thank you, thank you,' she said, and stopped, aware of burbling in her relief. 'I can continue to use the barn?'

'Yes, and to take your flowers from the garden.'

'Thank you,' Anya said again.

'Why is the village so special to you?' Garson enquired. 'Did you live here as a child? You don't have a local accent. You don't have any particular accent.'

'That's because until I came here I'd never lived anywhere longer than two years. My father was in the Army and his job meant that he was posted to a variety of locations both in this country and abroad,' she explained. 'Mostly my mother, my sister and I went with him, though if education was difficult we stayed behind, but the nomadic life meant that there was never enough time for us to make friends—real friends. We were a close family, but I always wanted to feel that I belonged somewhere and I never did.

'No, I didn't live in Lidden Magnor,' Anya said, finally replying to his question, 'but my parents rented a bungalow here one summer and I had golden memories of the village as a place which was calm and unchanging. When Oliver was a baby we lived with my uncle and aunt, but we couldn't stay there for ever so—'

'Wasn't there enough room?' Garson cut in.

'There was room. They have a large detached house and no children of their own, but they're a house-proud couple and, whilst they'd cooed over Oliver in his pram, once he started to walk and could put sticky fingers on the furniture and open cupboards, they were not amused. The atmosphere grew increasingly strained and a move became essential. But also—'

'Also what?' he asked, when she broke off to frown.

'Also although it'd been their idea that we should live with them I was always conscious of their silent disapproval of Oliver's existence.'

'They felt a husband was *de rigueur*?'

'Something like that,' Anya said tersely.

'You didn't consider renting somewhere near them?' Garson enquired.

'Yes, but my uncle works in the construction of hydroelectric dams and so he and his wife often have lengthy spells when they live abroad.'

'This is why they've gone to Brazil?'

She nodded. 'For two years. Anyway, I decided that rather than remaining in Yorkshire where they were the only temporary draw I'd make a life in Lidden Magnor. Oliver may not have much in the way of family,' Anya continued, 'but I've filled the gap with friends like Bert and Kirsten and Derek. And when my uncle and aunt are home I always take him to stay with them at Christmas and other holidays.' She gave a dry smile.

'Because it's just for a short time, they make an enormous fuss of him.'

'And you came here because you wanted to put down roots?' Garson enquired.

'Yes, and I want Oliver to have a solid sense of his own roots. I'd like him to be able to walk along the street and say hello to people he knows, and who know him. And when he's a man and perhaps moves away I want him to be able to return to the village and feel that it's home. I want him to *belong* and now he will.' Lifting up her glass, Anya raised it in a smiling toast. 'With my sincere gratitude for all your kindness.'

Garson reached for his own glass. 'To you and your son,' he responded.

As they drank the champagne, Anya was pensive. Should she tell him that Oliver was her nephew? she wondered. It would seem appropriate, in view of their new friendship. Indeed, their closeness made her want to share the truth and explain everything. She was deciding how best to start when Garson suddenly shifted his position at the other end of the sofa.

'It's Oliver I want to talk about,' he said, in a voice which sliced away his earlier hesitancy. 'You refused to allow him to call me Uncle and as one of his friends appears to have dubious uncles I understand why. However, I'm authentic.'

Anya looked at him in confusion. 'Authentic?' she repeated. 'An authentic uncle? What do you mean?'

Garson's blue eyes met hers in a steady gaze. 'I'm Lucan Cesari's brother.'

CHAPTER FIVE

'His brother?' Anya gave a startled hoot of laughter.
'What ever are you talking about? You can't be. Lucan
Cesari doesn't have a brother. He has two younger sisters
who—who dote on him and wait on him hand and foot
whenever he goes home,' she said, hastily recalling what
Jennie had told her about her lover, way back in the
past.

'Although he would've loved that, he didn't,' Garson
said. He hesitated, as if about to take issue with some
other facet of her denial, but then he continued, 'There
was just Luke and me.'

'You don't look like him,' Anya objected. She had
never met the pop singer in person, but she had seen
him on television. Slender, with black curls hanging
halfway down his back and limpid dark eyes, he had
been a romantic yet raunchy figure. 'Your features are
stronger and you're much more solidly built.'

'I take after my father's side of the family, whereas
most of his genes seemed to come from my mother.'

'But I thought Lucan Cesari was of Italian descent,'
she protested.

'My mother's a quarter Italian. His real name was
Luke,' Garson went on, 'but he didn't want to use his
own name professionally so he chose Lucan because it'd
always appealed and Cesari, which is our maternal
grandmother's family name.'

'Why would he say he had sisters if he hadn't?' Anya
demanded, using the query as a diversion to allow herself
time to think.

Minutes earlier she had been all set to divulge the truth of her relationship with Oliver, but no longer. Then everything had been safe and sure, she had had the Feel Good Factor oozing from every pore, but now... All of a sudden, her life with the little boy seemed threatened.

Panic gripped her. She sensed a minefield ahead and she must tread carefully, Anya cautioned herself. So she would allow Garson to continue to believe that she was Oliver's natural mother—her mind thrummed—which, in turn, meant she must act as if she was, and had been, Jennie. Though she did not understand why he should confuse her with her sister.

'In part because it was wishful thinking, but also because concocting a make-believe background helped dissociate him from our father and from me,' Garson replied. He cast her a look. 'I don't know how well you knew Luke—'

'Not well,' Anya inserted, at speed.

'—but you must've realised that he needed to be the centre of attention?'

'Mmm,' she said vaguely.

'And that included him being known as Lucan Cesari, period. Although he retired a long time ago, my father used to be a politician, but Luke would've hated being referred to in the media as "the son of Edwin Deverill, one-time Member of Parliament", or as my brother. He would've felt it detracted from *his* fame.' Rising, Garson crossed to the table and returned with the carrier bag. 'Here's the two of us together,' he said, producing an envelope and handing her a photograph. 'It was taken at a family gathering about a year ago.'

Garson and the pop star were standing in a sunny garden, grinning, with their arms slung fondly around each other's shoulders. Their physiques might have been different—Garson was a man, broad, strongly built, powerful, whilst Lucan Cesari remained a slender boy—yet, seeing them together, she saw similarities in the slant of their high cheekbones and the vital growth of their thick dark hair. The relationship was real. Anya's panic spiralled. But what consequences did it have for her and Oliver?

'Lucan Cesari has sent you here?' she demanded. For years she had nurtured the hope that one day his heart would soften and the young man would make contact with his son, but suddenly she was seized by a chilling terror. 'Now that Oliver's past the messy baby and toddler stage, he's decided to acknowledge his existence? It's too late. And if he's thinking of trying to obtain custody and retrieve him he's wasting his time. He has no claim. None!' Anya declared, yet although the word was fierce she was well aware that, as the little boy's father, Lucan Cesari *did* have a claim. A strong one.

Her heart quaked. But where did *she* stand?

'He didn't send me,' Garson said, and hesitated, frowning. 'He doesn't want custody.'

The immediacy of Anya's terror receded. 'But you came to Lidden Magnor to look for me?'

'For you and Oliver,' he said.

She put a hand to her head. Thoughts had begun bumping around in her brain like balls bumping around in a pinball machine, each one striking off in a different, jarring and entirely separate direction.

'When you asked me about Oliver's father, you knew who he was,' Anya said accusingly.

Garson nodded. 'Yes.'

'But you didn't know who I was when we first met. Hasn't Lucan Cesari told you what I look like?' she enquired. What Jennie looked like, she amended silently.

'Luke never mentioned you,' he said. 'Nor Oliver.'

Anya winced. Had her sister and her son been of so little interest to the singer?

'In that case, how did you know we existed?' she demanded. 'If he hasn't spoken of us, how did you know to come here?'

'Anya, I said never mentioned. Past tense. And I've been speaking of him in the past tense.' Garson's blue eyes were sombre. 'I'm sorry to have to tell you this but Luke is dead.'

'Dead?' She stared at him for a long, stunned moment. Poor little Oliver, she thought; he had never met his father and now he never would. 'That's dreadful,' she said, and needed to blink away tears.

'He was on holiday in the Caribbean with some friends and a speedboat they were in overturned. Luke suffered what's called a hangman's fracture and died within seconds, so he wouldn't have felt much pain,' Garson explained, as if attempting to offer her some crumb of comfort.

'When did this happen?' Anya asked.

'Back in February.' His brows drew together. 'I hadn't realised until just now that you didn't know and then telling you became . . . difficult.'

'I suppose that telling me who you were from the start was difficult too? I suppose it was easier to play games with me, to play false?' she demanded, resentment starting to build inside her. Her silence over her true status with Oliver was on the little boy's behalf and could be described as a benign deception, but Garson had deceived in a cold-blooded and calculating way. Her thoughts struck off in another direction. 'If Lucan Cesari never mentioned us, how come you recognised my name—surname,' she amended, 'when we first met?'

'A member of his band told me it. He said you went under the stage name of Vashti—'

'Oh—yes,' Anya said as she tardily recollected how the vocalist had insisted that Jennie must be called something more exotic.

'But he couldn't remember your Christian name, just that your family name was Prescott.'

Another ball bumped in her head. 'Oliver and I are the reason why you first took an interest in The Grange, aren't we?' she enquired.

Garson nodded. 'When I came at Easter—'

'When we were away.'

'—I saw that the house was for sale and pretending to be a buyer gave me an excuse to find out something about you and to come again. Though pressure of work meant that it was a while before I could return.'

'And when you did all your talk about wanting to know about the neighbours was double-talk!'

'I needed the information,' Garson said, his gaze level and unperturbed.

'When you came a second time and saw The Grange in the morning, you fixed an afternoon appointment to view the cottages and—' indignation flashed in her eyes '—to cross-examine me about my love life! You insisted on running me up to the school so that you could inspect Oliver,' Anya stormed on, 'and you bought The Grange because of us; though you didn't make the final decision until you'd seen him.'

'I had to be sure he was Luke's child and he's his miniature.'

'So you don't require him to take a blood test or have his DNA analysed?' she gibed. 'Let's be thankful for small mercies!'

'Do you have to be so aggressive?' Garson protested.

'Did you have to be so two-faced?' Anya slammed back. She recalled how leery he had been of her at the beginning—or had been of her twin, though it was one and the same thing. They had been close when Jennie was alive and she felt close to her now. She always would. Jennie had been a part of her, and vice versa. 'I assume that on the occasion when you suggested bed after coffee you were testing my moral fibre?'

Garson pursed his lips. 'In part.'

'Only in part? You mean you would've made love to me if I'd been willing?'

'I can't say.' His eyes flickered over her. 'But you are a most desirable woman.'

Anya ignored his last remark—and the frisson which it had created. She refused to be sidetracked. 'What surprises me,' she said blisteringly, 'is that instead of hiring a team of private detectives to do your dirty work for you you went through all the hassle and spent so much time acting the sleuth yourself. But congratulations, you've done an excellent job of spying and investigating. And, even better, in the process you've managed to endear yourself to Oliver and—' hurt and resentment glittered in her eyes '—to ingratiate yourself with me.'

'Ingratiate?' he queried.

'By getting me so involved in The Grange, and paying a much welcomed salary, and by kissing me earlier this evening. I was under the impression we were developing a rapport—' Anya gave a brittle laugh '—but you were simply softening me up before you made your grand announcement.'

'You can't believe that,' Garson said, his voice thick with protest.

'Can't I?' Anya no longer knew what she believed; she only knew that she felt used and cheated and tricked. Tricked by a man whom she had begun to like, very much. By a man who had seemed special. By a man whom she had almost given herself to—willingly and so unsuspectingly. 'You once reckoned you liked to come

straight to the point, so how is it you took such a de-
vious roundabout route before confessing who you really
were?' she demanded.

His reply was terse. 'I had no choice.'

'What you chose,' she snapped, 'was to deceive me!'

Anya needed to snap and be angry, otherwise she might
have burst into tears. And once she started to cry it would
be difficult to stop.

'I couldn't tell you who I was because I had no idea
of the kind of person you were,' Garson said heavily.

'But you thought the worst.' The look she flung him
was acidic. 'You'd marked me down as a tramp.'

'I've given you a full apology for that,' he said, his
tone impatient.

'But you're not going to apologise for deceiving me
because it gave you no struggles with your conscience?'
she taunted. 'Not one pinprick of doubt? Of shame?
Well, just you listen—'

Garson cut her off. 'No, *you* listen. You listen while
I tell you the whole story and then you'll understand.'

Anya glowered. 'Will I?'

'*Yes!*'

She had said—and so had he—that he would cope in
the face of her fury, she remembered, and with his blue
eyes steely and his manner forceful Garson was coping
fine. Roger Adlam might have slunk meekly away, but
he was a different, far tougher animal.

She shone him a bloodless smile. 'Please, go ahead.'

'Thank you,' Garson said brusquely. He was silent
for a moment or two as if organising his thoughts, and
when he spoke again his tone was reasoned and
reasonable. 'As my parents are elderly and were extremely distressed by Luke's death, I handled the fu-
neral arrangements and afterwards cleared his belongings
out of his apartment.'

'Was he still living in the Docklands penthouse, over-looking the river?' Anya enquired, matching her tone to his.

No matter how deceived she might feel, she knew that not only, in all fairness, ought she to listen to what Garson had to say, but also that she *needed* to listen. She needed to know why he had sought out her and Oliver. If he had established and maintained contact, then he had something in mind. Anxiety gnawed in the pit of her stomach. The masterful Mr Deverill had a game plan.

'He was,' Garson replied. 'The rent'd become more than he could afford, but my father made up the shortfall. Luke may not have had doting sisters, but—' his voice was dry '—he did have doting parents.'

'There must've been a sizeable gap in age between the two of you,' she remarked.

'Ten years.'

'Was he an afterthought?'

Garson smiled. 'No, Luke was a gift from heaven. My parents had had me as soon as they decided to start a family, but when they wanted a second child it was three or four years before my mother became pregnant again and then she miscarried,' he explained. 'There was a further similar wait, another pregnancy, another mis-carriage. By this time they'd become desperate and when the doctors said that my mother's age meant she had little chance of conceiving again they took it hard.'

He hesitated, his face sombre, as if he understood and sympathised. 'They wondered about adoption, but they were both well into their forties and failed to meet the agencies' criteria. Then, a couple of years on, my mother miraculously became pregnant again and, lo and behold, Luke was born.'

'What did you feel about having a brother after you'd been the only child for so long?' Anya enquired. She was a sucker for family sagas and now she could not resist being drawn into the tale.

'I was thankful. My mother has a passion for motherhood and adores kids, but by the age of ten I was finding her adoration increasingly irritating. I needed freedom to grow up and Luke provided it. She ran round in circles looking after him and my father was besotted too. They'd been firm with me, but they were so over-joyed to have Luke that they spoiled him rotten.' Garson gave a rueful smile. 'Though he was a most attractive little kid—energetic, inquisitive, bright as a button, like Oliver. He was a charismatic guy when he grew up, too.'

Anya had detected a slight hesitation in his voice. 'Is there a but?'

'I'm afraid so,' he said, and frowned. 'Because the very first record Luke's band ever made shot straight to number one in the charts—'

'It did?' she said, in surprise.

'You didn't know?' he protested. 'But Luke and his pals were forever crowing about it, even years later.'

'Must've slipped my mind,' Anya said hastily.

Garson regarded her in silence for a moment. 'Luke's instant success meant he went straight from being the wunderkind at home to being idolised by thousands of fans,' he continued, 'and he didn't have the maturity to handle it. Hell, he was only twenty. Up to that point, if he was being a pain in the neck he could be joked out of it, but he committed the ultimate pop sin of believing his own publicity. Luke started to act the big I Am and, whilst the charisma always remained, he developed a ruthlessly selfish streak.' He shot her a glance. 'Which you must've realised.'

'I did,' she said tartly. 'I know he could be a bastard.'

Garson nodded. 'Much as I loved my brother, I have to admit that you're right. When I was going through his papers I came across this photograph of a baby,' he said, dipping into the envelope again, 'which gives your change of address on the back and says that it's Luke's son on his first birthday.'

'There was just a single photograph?' Anya asked, when he passed it to her. 'I sent him one taken on Oliver's birthday every year and I also sent him letters—several over the years.'

Garson moved his shoulders. 'They must've got lost.'

Or Lucan Cesari threw them away, possibly unopened, she thought astringently.

'Because having women claiming that they're the father of their child appears to be an occupational hazard where rock stars are concerned, at first I didn't take the photo seriously,' he continued. 'The baby may have had big dark eyes like Luke, but it didn't mean anything and there was no evidence of any follow-up. However, the photo kept nagging at me, so much so that eventually I tracked down Jason Walker—'

'Who?'

'Jason Walker. He played guitar with the band. A skinny, red-headed guy with a ponytail.' Garson thrust her a quizzical look. 'Surely you remember him?'

Anya flushed. 'Oh, yes, yes. I do now,' she said.

'I asked him whether Luke had been involved with any particular girl at around the time of what would've been the baby's conception and he promptly said yes, Vashti Prescott. Jason told me that if I played the video of the band's last big hit I'd see her and when I ran my mother's much worn copy there you were—in a white boob tube and black miniskirt, swinging your hips and gyrating in the background.' Garson arched a brow. 'Most provocative.'

She ignored the comment; he was referring to her twin. 'So why didn't you recognise me when we first met?' she asked, puzzled.

'Because in the video you had short spiky blonde hair.'

One beat went by, and two. 'That's right,' Anya said, cursing herself for having forgotten about Jennie's dramatic change of appearance.

'You looked so different that I found it difficult to believe it was the same girl. I assume you wore a wig?'

'No.'

Garson eyed the tawny brown wisps which curled around her face and the luxuriant plait which lay over one shoulder. 'But you have beautiful hair; how could you chop it off and bleach it?' he protested, in a voice which condemned her action.

'Easy,' Anya said, for her sister had told her how, when Lucan Cesari had asked her to have an urchin cut and go platinum—so that she would contrast with the other girl dancer, who was Asian—she had been so much in love that she would have done anything to please him. In fact, Jennie had sped off to the hair salon the very same day. 'And you thought *I* was easy,' she said, returning to the attack and intent on defending her twin.

He stroked a pensive finger across the sculpted fullness of his lower lip. 'I thought all kinds of things.'

'Such as?' she demanded.

'I wondered if you might've been blackmailing Luke.'

'*What?*'

'Anya, by the time Luke died almost all of the money he'd earned in the past had disappeared, so—'

'He wasn't still having hits?' she cut in.

Garson shook his head. 'The band broke up around three years ago, at which point Luke embarked on a solo career which never took off.' He frowned. 'You didn't keep track of what was happening to him?'

Anya's colour rose again. If she had had a relationship with the vocalist she supposed she would have
shown more interest, but pretending to be Jennie held
more pitfalls than she had imagined.

'No,' she replied.

'Whilst Luke was perfectly capable of frittering the
money away,' Garson said, returning to his explanation,
'I did wonder whether you could've been a chick falsely
claiming that the baby was his and keen to feather her
nest by—perhaps—threatening to sell her kiss-and-tell
story to the Press.'

'Thanks!' The word was indignant.

'These things happen,' Garson said tersely.

'Maybe,' Anya was forced to concede. 'But then you
saw how I lived, which knocked the idea of any feather-
ing of a nest for six.'

'Yes, though you could already have spent the money.'

'On what?'

He moved a hand. 'Perhaps on super de luxe holidays
with a boyfriend.'

'And when you couldn't find any evidence of a boyfriend you wondered if I was going all out to trap Roger
and grab his cash—as I might've grabbed Lucan
Cesari's.' Anya shot him a rebellious look. 'Because a
girl has blonde hair and dances with a pop group, it
doesn't mean she's amoral or on the make.'

'You wondered if I wanted Jacuzzis and gold taps at
The Grange.'

'So?'

'You were making assumptions and pigeon-holing me,
wrongly, as I made assumptions about you. Also
wrongly.'

'I didn't accuse you of being a—a whore!' Anya
burst out.

'Look, you'd had an affair with Luke,' Garson said impatiently, 'which made me think—' He stopped dead.

'Made you think what?' she asked.

He frowned, as though he had been indiscreet and was regretting it. 'How much do you know about his previous girlfriends—or the ones who came after you?'

'Nothing.'

'Well, let's just say that Luke was none too discriminating in his choice of partners.'

'None too discriminating?' Anya enquired.

Garson looked at her. 'You don't want me to spell it out?' he protested.

'I do.'

He hesitated, massaging his jaw with a reluctant hand. 'I know that at least a couple of the girls took drugs and one was married with kids. But all were shallow and superficial, bimbos who'd sidled up to Luke because he was a celebrity and had money. So it seemed likely you'd be the same. I'm sorry, but—'

Anya sighed. 'I understand.' There was a moment or two of silence. 'What happens next?' she enquired, and her tone sharpened. 'Now that you've found Oliver and me, what do you have in mind?'

'I want to introduce him to my parents.'

The golden flecks glittered in her eyes. 'Go to hell!'

'He'd enjoy meeting them and they'd be delighted to meet him,' Garson said.

Anya's stomach began to pitch and toss. The spiralling panic returned. Her relationship, her rights to Oliver suddenly seemed horribly fragile.

'By buying The Grange, which means you're my landlord, and by employing me, which makes me feel indebted, I suppose you think you've manoeuvred me into a corner?' she demanded. 'Sorry, I refuse to be cornered—or trapped.'

'Trapped?'

'Meeting your parents could be a trap. Once they've seen Oliver and been enchanted they might decided that they have a stronger claim on him than me. Your parents—represented by *you*—might attempt to prise him away,' Anya declared as scenes of a court case and a screaming Oliver being forcibly wrenched from her created a maelstrom of bristling emotions in her head.

'That's absurd,' Garson said.

'Is it?' Sweeping to her feet, Anya flung a hand towards the door. 'Get out of here!'

'Keep your voice down—you'll wake Oliver,' he protested.

'Go!' she spat.

Garson did not move. 'I'm not going until we've talked this through, calmly and sensibly,' he said, crossing one long leg over the other and resting back as if he was prepared to sit on the sofa for all eternity.

'I don't want to talk! There's nothing to talk about. I'm going to bed. Right this minute,' Anya announced impetuously. 'And if you follow me upstairs I shall scream, which will alarm Oliver and—'

'If I follow you upstairs, we'll end up in bed together,' he said, in a low baritone. 'You know it and I know it.'

Her heart thudded. 'Do I?' Anya said, but the query which she had intended to be a challenge sounded woefully uncertain.

'You may consider me to be an arch villain who sleeps in a coffin,' Garson said, 'but you still lust after me. And I lust after you. I never thought I'd fancy a woman whom Luke had fancied, but—' He broke off suddenly to frown. 'Jason said you went with the band on their European tour and that lasted for—what, four months?'

'Right,' Anya agreed, though she could not precisely recall the timescale.

Around the period of her sister's romance she had been sitting her finals, graduating from university and finding herself a job, and had been too busy with her own life to monitor Jennie's activities too closely.

'Yet you didn't remember Jason and you reckon you didn't know Luke well? And you obviously know damn all about his past,' Garson muttered. Creases crept across his forehead. 'You've continually referred to Luke as Lucan Cesari—why? Even though the relationship did end badly, the two of you were once lovers.'

Anya felt her cheeks fill with heat. What could she say? She was not very good at telling lies, especially when placed under the scrutiny of such a sharp-eyed interrogator. When she failed to reply, Garson got to his feet and walked over to stand in front of her.

'You were lovers?' he repeated, but this time the words formed a question. 'Oliver *is* Luke's son?'

'Yes, he is.'

'But?'

The tip of her tongue sneaked out to moisten her lips. She needed time to consider the implications of the new situation he had presented her with. Time to weigh up the dangers, and decide how best to handle them—and until she did surely it would be wise to hold onto her secret? Mightn't it act as a bargaining tool? Yes. Yet holding on had risks, Anya thought frantically. All it would need was for Oliver to decide to confide in his 'friend', Mr Deverill, and—

'You have a sister,' Garson slowly, thoughtfully.

She took a breath. He was too clever. 'I had a twin sister.'

'Had?' he queried.

Anya nodded. 'Jennie was Oliver's mother, but she died when he was a week old and I've cared for him ever since.'

'Oh, God,' Garson said, in a stricken voice. 'Then it was your twin whom I saw on the video?'

'Yes, and it was Jennie who chopped off her hair and—' her look was lethal '—Jennie whom you thought might be a tramp.'

He considered this. 'But it was *you* who deceived me,' he said quietly, 'which makes us equal. As our link with Oliver—me being his uncle and you being his aunt—is also equal.'

Anya frowned. Did the bond which had formed so easily between Garson and the little boy have anything to do with their blood tie? she wondered.

'I agree with your second statement, but not with the first,' she told him. 'Your deception was a deliberately contrived cat-and-mouse strategy, whereas any fudging of the facts which I've done has been to protect Oliver.'

'He believes that you're his mother?' Garson asked.

'No, he knows his mother was Jennie,' she said, and explained how she had told him. 'But so far as I'm aware Oliver has never revealed the truth to anyone. He may well decide to do so in the future, but for now keeping quiet seems to give him emotional security. I've told friends, like Kirsten, in confidence, but until Oliver's willing for the situation to become common knowledge I intend to keep quiet too.'

'You fooled me,' he remarked.

'Ditto. For three months you've been acting a sham while you checked us out right, left and centre,' Anya said, her resentment gathering again. 'And now you think you can steer me into a meeting with your parents, just like you've so cleverly steered me into everything else? Well, you may have endeared and ingratiated, and be completely impervious to *my* feelings, and to any shame or embarrassment, but there's no way you'll steer me into anything ever again!'

'Have you finished?' Garson enquired.

She glared at him. 'I've finished.'

'Then, whilst I can't blame you for seeing it differently, what I did was spend three months establishing that you're a reliable and responsible person and, at the same time, letting you know that I'm reliable and responsible too.'

'And now you'd like a standing ovation?' Anya scythed.

'I thought you said you'd finished?'

She shone him an ersatz smile. 'Sorry.'

'Which was necessary before I brought everyone together, for your peace of mind as well as mine,' Garson continued. 'If I've endeared myself to Oliver, he's endeared himself to me too. He's a super kid and you've done a great job of bringing him up.'

'How kind,' Anya said tightly, though she was warmed by the compliment.

'Have you adopted Oliver?' he enquired.

'Why do you want to know?' she demanded, suddenly on red alert. 'What difference does it make? I may not be his biological mother but I'm the next best thing and for five years I've—'

'Cool it,' Garson commanded. 'Whether you've adopted him or not, no one's going to attempt to prise Oliver away from you. Not my parents, not me, not anyone.' He returned to the sofa. 'Come and sit down,' he said, patting the seat beside him.

Anya hesitated, then walked across to sit down again, though keeping as far away from him as possible.

'No, I haven't adopted Oliver,' she said. 'When he was a baby I wondered whether I should, but I was only twenty-three, a single girl with no home of my own, intermittent family support and limited funds, and I wasn't sure whether the powers that be would consider me a suitable guardian.'

'You feared the answer might be negative?' Garson enquired.

She nodded. 'So I decided to wait until my suitability had been established with years of successful caring and—' her brow creased '—I've yet to get around to setting the adoption process in motion.'

'When you do, there should be no problem.'

'I shouldn't think so,' Anya agreed.

'God knows, I'm not impervious to your feelings,' he said, returning to her earlier comment, 'and I'd never ask you to do anything against your will. My only wish is that Oliver and my folks should have a chance to meet, but there's no steering.'

She frowned. Her refusal to so much as contemplate a meeting—and the demand that Garson must leave—had been impulsive, an instinctive response to panic and fear. But her fear was receding.

'Have you already told your parents to expect a visit?' Anya enquired.

'No. They aren't even aware of Oliver's existence. And, whilst knowing about him would provide much comfort, I shan't tell them unless you give your permission.'

'I don't.'

Garson spread his hands. 'Your choice.'

'Even if Oliver doesn't have the usual quota of relatives, he's perfectly happy,' Anya said, beset by an urgent though annoying need to defend her decision.

'I don't deny that, though his wish to acquire an uncle would appear to indicate that he feels he's missing out in some way. My parents feel that by not having a grandchild they're missing out too,' he told her, and paused, his expression becoming inscrutable. 'I've been married—'

'To Isobel Dewing, the TV presenter, I know,' she said.

'And when I didn't produce any children my folks set their hopes on Luke, and now his death makes Oliver all the more precious. Losing him brought them low and has taken its toll, but seeing Oliver would be a tremendous boost.'

Anya felt torn two ways. 'This is emotional blackmail,' she protested.

'It is,' Garson agreed.

She frowned at him. 'Is there nothing you wouldn't stoop to?'

'No, not when there's something I want, something which I know is *right*,' he replied. 'Hell, Anya, it's clear that you care deeply about Oliver—about his happiness and his sense of belonging—so why deprive him of his grandparents? My folks live in Winchester, which isn't much more than an hour's drive from here. I could ring them and explain everything, and we could take Oliver over for lunch on Sunday.'

'This is why you decided to have a four-day break here this time?' Anya enquired.

He nodded. 'As I was driving from the airport I thought of how, when I last telephoned, my mother'd said she wished Luke could've left a child, and I decided I couldn't wait any longer. I had to act. Dammit, I have to *try*,' he insisted, bringing his hand down flat on the low table with such force that their glasses jumped.

'You're so scheming, I don't know how you can live with yourself,' she remarked, though her tone was dry rather than abrasive.

Garson grinned. 'I manage.'

'What about The Grange?' she asked curiously. 'Have the renovations merely been an exercise in involving yourself with us or do you intend to use the house?'

'At first they were a means of involvement, but now—' He gave a crooked smile. 'I look forward to getting away from the hurly-burly and coming down to Dorset. The prospect of spending weekends in the country has a definite appeal.' He fixed her with steady blue eyes. 'As does taking you and Oliver over to Winchester.'

'Do you never let up?' Anya protested.

'Nope. I believe in try, try and try again.'

She chewed fretfully at her lip. 'Before Oliver met your parents—*if* he met them—I'd need to tell him who his father was.'

'He doesn't know?' Garson enquired.

'He knows he was a musician, but he isn't aware that he was Lucan Cesari, the rock star, and, at this stage, I'd prefer it if he didn't. It would mean other people getting to know and maybe gossiping. The Press could even pick up on it.'

'I see no problem. We just say his father was Luke Deverill and I ask my folks to keep quiet about Luke's fame.'

'I'd also have to explain to Oliver that his father's dead,' Anya continued, her face growing troubled, 'and it might upset him.'

'If he's told with sensitivity he'll be fine,' Garson assured her, 'and we can tell him together.'

'But we wouldn't say that Lucan—Luke,' she adjusted, 'refused to do the decent thing and accept his paternity. Despite knowing that Jennie was a virgin who had slept only with him.'

He muttered an oath beneath his breath. 'I'm not attempting to excuse my brother—I've agreed he could be a bastard—but he was young and the idea of becoming a father probably frightened him. Also the pop fans don't care for their idols to have families, so he may've thought that accepting Oliver would mean the end of his career.'

'I suppose,' Anya acknowledged.

'Did it never occur to your sister that Luke wasn't the wisest choice of partner?' Garson asked.

'Apparently not; she seemed to totally misread his character.'

'We can all make that mistake,' he said heavily.

'But she met him not long after our parents had died, when she was lost and vulnerable,' Anya said, leaping to her twin's defence. 'Unfortunately the bank where Jennie was a trainee had just cut its staff when the accident happened, so she was out of a job. She had too much time to think and she sat in the house on her own, remembering Mum and Dad and becoming more and more depressed.'

'You were at university?' Garson enquired.

Anya nodded. 'Mum and Dad being killed was traumatic for me too, but my finals were approaching and being forced to study stopped me from brooding too much. Also, I'd been away from home for three years, whereas Jennie had always lived with our parents, so she missed them on a daily basis, which made things even worse.'

'How did she meet Luke?'

'A neighbour's son who worked as a roadie with rock groups dragged her along to one of his concerts to cheer her up and afterwards he introduced them. It was just before the band were due to set off on tour and a dancer had quit, and when Luke saw Jennie he offered her the job.'

'She'd trained as a dancer?'

'No, so she was astonished by the suggestion. But Luke insisted that all she needed to do was look sexy and swing her hips, and she agreed. She had nothing else lined up and she reckoned joining a pop group was preferable to moping around at home.'

Anya gave a whimsical smile. 'Jennie soon discovered that she had a flair for bumping and grinding. She also discovered that she loved being on tour. She said moving around *en masse* created a great feeling of companionship and that, from being adrift, she felt as if she was a member of a family again. Luke had made it happen so he seemed like her saviour and I think that's a big part of why she fell in love with him.'

'Then one night they got . . . careless,' Garson said.

'Several nights they were careless; apparently Luke preferred it that way,' Anya said tartly. 'But he always maintained that nothing would happen and, as Jennie was scared of spoiling their relationship and putting her job with the band at risk, she chose to believe him. However, my sister was *not* shallow or superficial,' she insisted. 'She was not a groupie and although she may have chosen to inhabit a freewheeling world it didn't mean she was a freewheeler herself.'

'There's no need to be so fiercely protective,' he demurred, and frowned at her. 'Did your uncle and aunt regard Jennie as a freewheeler?'

She gave a wan smile. 'Yes. They couldn't understand how desperate she'd been for comfort. I tried to explain, but they always implied that Jennie should've had more sense and that the consequences were her own silly fault.'

'I understand,' Garson said.

Anya shot him a wary look. Did he? Did he sympathise?

'Three months into their affair, Jennie discovered she was pregnant,' she continued, 'but when she told Luke he immediately declared that the child wasn't his, refused point-blank to discuss the matter and, from then on, ignored her.'

'For God's sake!' Garson rasped.

'Quite. Jennie couldn't believe it. Because she was convinced that, given time, he must accept the truth she stayed on with the band, but he continued to ignore her and so eventually she left.'

'And she decided to keep the baby?'

'She *wanted* to keep it,' Anya said. 'She loved Luke and there was no way she would've terminated his child. Jennie loved him until the day she died,' she said, and shook a wondering head. 'Crazy, wasn't it?'

Garson looked at her. 'No matter how much someone hurts you, you can still continue to love them. For ever,' he said soberly.

'I guess. When she had Oliver, Jennie needed a Caesarian and afterwards she suffered internal haemorrhaging.' Anya swallowed. Her throat had stiffened and tears were welling at the back of her eyes. 'The doctors said it was a million to one tragedy, but she died.'

He reached out to place a hand comfortingly over hers. 'First you lost your parents and then your sister. You really went through it.'

'Yes.' She swallowed again. 'But Oliver was the hope for the future and I loved him the minute I saw him and—' she shone him a watery smile '—you know the rest.'

Garson held her hand until she had recovered and then he sat back. 'You must've wished that your parents could've known Jennie's child and that he could've known them,' he said.

'Many times,' Anya acknowledged.

'So do we go to Winchester?'

She linked her hands tight in her lap. 'Yes, but only on the understanding that it's a trial run and that if Oliver should be disturbed in any way it won't be repeated. I'm sorry if that seems harsh on your parents, but Oliver's well-being is of paramount importance to me and must come first. You agree?' Anya demanded.

'I agree,' Garson said, 'but he won't be disturbed. Trust me.'

CHAPTER SIX

'THIS is one of the happiest days of my life,' Dulcie Deverill declared, gazing out at the lawn where Oliver was kicking a ball around with his grandfather. 'To see our darling Luke living on in that precious child is—' she clasped her hands together and sighed '—like a dream come true.'

After a lunch of melon, grilled salmon, followed by strawberries and cream, their hostess had ushered everyone back through to the comfortably furnished drawing room. Coffee had been served and, on swiftly drinking his, Edwin Deverill had suggested that Oliver might like to go out into the garden and play with the football which had been bought specially. The old man had claimed that this was to prevent the little boy becoming bored, though Anya suspected that his real aim had been to spend time with his grandson on his own.

Rising, Garson strolled across to lean a broad shoulder against the lintel of the open French doors and watch the game. 'I thought my father suffered from arthritis,' he remarked, grinning as the tall, stooped figure executed some surprisingly nimble footwork. 'Oliver seems to have cured it.'

'He's cured so many things,' Dulcie said, sighing again. She smiled at Anya. 'Would you mind if I showed him some photographs of Luke when he was small? I don't want to upset him, but—'

'I'm sure he'd love to see them,' Anya replied, thinking that Oliver had not been upset by anything.

It was true that yesterday he had cried when she had told him that his daddy had died, but his tears had been short-lived. This had been because Garson had gone on to explain that he was his daddy's brother and thus his uncle.

'My uncle?' Oliver had said, rapidly scrubbing his cheeks dry. He had stood in front of the sofa where his hero was sitting. 'So I can call you Uncle Garson?'

'You can,' Garson had replied, and lifted him onto his lap. 'And I shall call you Nephew Oliver.'

The little boy had giggled. 'Don't be silly. You don't call people Nephew.'

'You're right. But you do call them Grandpa and Grandma,' he had said, with a look at Anya.

'And tomorrow we're going to see your grandpa and grandma,' she had told him, picking up her cue, and together she and Garson had explained.

When they had arrived at the elegant stone villa on the outskirts of Winchester both Dulcie and Edwin Deverill had wept—though, not wishing Oliver to see, their tears had been concealed and quickly wiped away. Anya had almost wept too. The old couple had been so grateful for the meeting and Oliver, the only one whose composure had remained sturdy—for Garson's eyes had looked suspiciously damp—had been so excited.

There had been no sign of shyness, just wide-eyed fascination with the aristocratic, grey zapata-moustached gentleman and the effusive, silver-haired, rather frail old lady who were his grandparents. And, as with Garson, an instant bond had formed. Within minutes the little boy had been leaning against Edwin's knee, calling him Grandpa as if he had always done so and telling him how he had another grandad, Bert.

'Only he's not a proper one, like you are,' Oliver had said, beaming triumphantly up at the old man, and everyone's eyes had dampened again.

As she collected albums from a bureau, Dulcie looked back at Anya. 'I also have pictures of Garson's wedding,' she said, darting a glance at her son and lowering her voice as though if he overheard what she was saying he might object. 'He looked so handsome in his morning suit and Isobel was beautiful.'

'I can imagine,' Anya replied, with a smile, but, as she visualised the bride and groom on their wedding day, her smile became strained.

With her smooth ashen hair, heart-shaped face and flawless complexion, Isobel Dewing would have been not just beautiful, but breathtaking. A gracious princess, she thought, and felt a spurt of jealousy which was as physical and painful as heartburn.

Anya drank the last mouthful of her coffee. Yet why should she be jealous? Garson's wedding had taken place a long time ago, he had been married to a woman she did not know, and now the marriage had ended. Besides, she had no claim on him—nor wanted one. They might lust after each other, but lust was an unreliable physical feeling and a long way from love.

'Isobel has such marvellous taste in clothes,' the old lady continued, speaking in confidential and admiring tones. 'I know her wedding dress cost the earth, but it was so elegant and yet so chic. Mind you, Isobel's the kind of woman who makes whatever she wears look expensive.'

Anya put down her cup and saucer. All of a sudden, she was horribly aware that her white cotton shirt and high-waisted *café au lait* trousers had been bought in a chain store and could probably be recognised as such. It did not matter that, like Garson, who wore a polo shirt and blue jeans, she had chosen to come casually dressed; she felt plain and nondescript.

Dulcie placed the albums on the coffee-table. 'I know you never met Luke, but perhaps you'd like to see the pictures of him as a child too?' she suggested, her voice rising.

Anya forced a smile. Right now, she did not feel in the mood for looking at *any* photographs, not of someone whom she regarded as the quintessential rotter—even if he had had his reasons and even though his mother did adore him—and certainly not of Isobel. But how could she refuse? She was searching for an excuse when Garson turned from the French windows.

'Why don't we go for a walk and leave my mother to show Oliver the photographs?' he suggested. 'He'll be fine here.'

'Yes, Edwin and I will be delighted to look after him,' Dulcie put in eagerly.

Anya rose to her feet. 'What a good idea,' she said.

With Oliver installed on the sofa beside his grand- mother, happily listening to the fond reminiscences which accompanied each picture, they departed.

'You said you'd never been to Winchester before,' Garson remarked as they set off down a tree-lined avenue towards the town, 'so I'll take you to the cathedral—' he indicated a tower which soared high above the roofs '—and on to the Great Hall.'

Anya nodded her agreement, and for a minute or two they walked along in silence. It was a warm day and, below them at the foot of the hill, the clustered buildings glowed golden in the rays of the early August sunshine.

'How long were you married?' she enquired.

She had never given much thought to the relationship before, but Dulcie's reference to his wife had sparked off her curiosity.

'Four years,' Garson replied. A muscle tightened in his jaw. 'My mother was very fond of Isobel and, although I've told her it won't happen, she clings onto the hope that the two of us might get back together again.'

'Isobel hasn't become involved with anyone else?'

'She's playing at sweethearts with some programme controller,' he said tersely, and squinted against the sunshine. 'Or, at least, she was the last time we spoke.'

'You keep in touch?' Anya asked.

'It must be three years or more since we last met,' he said, his eyes trained ahead, 'but when we separated Isobel took the house we were living in in settlement and she occasionally rings me with a query about it.'

Aware of veering towards the overly intrusive and yet suddenly desperate to know, Anya cast him a glance. 'Why did your marriage go wrong?'

'Incompatability,' Garson replied.

She frowned. 'Incompatability' was the kind of catch-all term which professed to say everything when, in fact, it said nothing. But one thing was certain—he did not approve of his ex-wife dating. If her theory about Isobel Dewing leaving because he had devoted too much time to his work and too little to her was accurate, did Garson regret this? Anya wondered as they walked along. Might he have offered to change his ways and been advised that it was too late? Like his mother, did he hope that the relationship could be revived?

She longed to ask, but the grim set of his mouth warned that his marriage had become a no-go area and all she would get in reply would be another short and evasive answer.

After admiring the splendours of the ancient cathedral which contained the grave of Jane Austen, the famous novelist, Garson shepherded her away across wide green lawns and through a smartly pedestrianised shopping area.

'The Great Hall is the only visible remaining part of what was once a medieval castle,' he explained as they walked into an open square. He gestured towards the building which squatted ahead of them. 'Richard Coeur de Lion returned here in 1194 to await his coronation in the cathedral and almost five hundred years later the castle was captured by Oliver Cromwell during the Civil War.'

'You know your history,' Anya commented.

Garson grinned. 'That's because the Great Hall's always fascinated me.'

When they went inside the lofty aisled building, she could understand his fascination for here several different ages of history were intriguingly melded together. A bronze statue of Queen Victoria stood majestically to one side, at the end of the Hall she saw intricate stainless-steel gates which had been erected to commemorate the marriage in 1981 of the Prince and Princess of Wales, while the stained-glass windows dated from the last century.

But it was the table hung high on the far wall which gripped Anya's interest. Painted in the Tudor colours of green and white, inscriptions showed a king surrounded by twenty-four of his knights.

'That's King Arthur's Round Table?' she said, in surprise. 'I wasn't aware that it existed.'

'Whether this table was actually used by Arthur seems to be uncertain, but it's hung here for five hundred years. You see the eleventh knight?' Garson said, pointing to the inscription.

'Lucan,' Anya read. 'That's where your brother took the name from?'

He nodded. 'He always fancied it as a kid, though he wasn't exactly a knight in shining armour,' he remarked drily.

'No chance. What about you? You've never been tempted to call yourself Galahad or Guinglain or Blioberis?' she enquired, her hazel eyes dancing as she mischieviously selected names.

Garson chuckled. 'No, I'm happy with the name I have—which is an old family name. Why did your sister choose Vashti for a stage name?' he asked suddenly.

'She didn't, Luke did. Apparently it comes from the Persian for beautiful and he told her she was beautiful.'

'Like you,' Garson said.

Anya smiled. Perhaps she did not look *so* plain in her chain-store clothes after all.

'Jennie chose Oliver because it means symbol of peace,' she carried on, then swung him a frowning glance. 'What did you tell your folks about my sister and Luke?'

'What you told me. How your parents had died and Jennie was feeling lost, and—'

'They understood?'

'They don't think she was a flighty piece or a groupie, if that's what you mean,' Garson replied, sounding impatient. 'Though they found it hard to accept that Luke could be so cruel. To be honest, I doubt my mother has accepted it; she tends to hear only what she wants to hear about him. As for my father—well, he became philosophical about Luke's bad behaviour long ago.' He checked his watch. 'We'd better be getting back.'

'This is the happiest day of my life,' Oliver declared. Lying back on the pillow, he rubbed small fists into his eyes. 'The bestest,' he said tiredly.

Anya smiled. Although the little boy was repeating a statement which he had heard his grandmother say several times, he meant it. She could not remember him ever looking so blissful or so relaxed. She felt relaxed too, she reflected as she drew the duvet up to his chin. She had particularly enjoyed the journey back in the car, when, with Oliver half-asleep on the back seat, she and Garson had talked over the day. Anyone seeing them chatting so easily together and noticing the drowsy child would have assumed they were a family heading home.

Her smile faltered. But they were not a family, she thought, and felt a pang. Being with Garson today had made her realise, with a startling clarity, that she wanted to share her life. Needed to share it. She needed—she *craved*—the feeling of closeness and companionship and belonging which they had shared. And so did Oliver. Now that they had both had a taste of what they were missing, existing as a single-parent family was no longer enough.

'I want my uncle Garson to kiss me as well,' the little boy declared, after she had kissed him goodnight.

'Yessir,' Anya said, and went to the top of the stairs. Instead of dropping them off and carrying on to The King's Head as she had expected, their chauffeur had suggested that he make cups of coffee while she put Oliver to bed. 'If it's possible, the little horror would like a kiss,' she called down, and heard a giggle behind her.

Garson came bounding up the stairs, his long legs taking them two at a time. 'It's possible,' he said.

After being kissed and declaring, once more, that it had been his very 'bestest' day, Oliver nestled down with his teddy bear beneath the covers.

'We're going to go to my grandpa and grandma's house again?' he checked.

'Soon,' Anya told him.

Obviously regarding Garson as their spokesman and deferring to him, the old couple had refrained from making any mention of a second meeting, but when they had been leaving Oliver had demanded to know if—please—they could visit another time. As Dulcie and Edwin had swung anxious eyes to her, Anya had agreed, and it was arranged that Garson would check his schedule and give them a call. Then a date would be fixed, either for another lunch at Winchester or for his parents to drive over to Lidden Magnor.

Satisfied with her assurance, Oliver yawned and closed his eyes. 'Night, night.'

'Goodnight,' she and Garson replied, in unison.

'My shoes have begun to nip and I want to change them,' Anya said as they went out onto the landing and she closed Oliver's door. 'I'll be down in a minute.'

Swinging into her room, she eased the beige leather pumps from her feet. She made a face. There was a hole in the toe of her tights which, if she left them on, would grow larger. Anya had shed her trousers and was sitting on the bed peeling off the tights, when she saw a shape at the edge of her vision. Her heart missed a beat. Garson was standing on the landing. His gaze was flickering over the smoothness of her thighs and down the shapely length of her bare legs.

'I thought you'd gone to see to the coffee,' she said.

His gaze lifted to hers. 'I prefer to watch you,' he said huskily.

Stretching forward, Anya lifted the lid on the wicker laundry basket and dropped her tights inside. Isobel Dewing might be chic and elegant, yet the undisguised male interest which she saw in Garson's eyes said that she possessed her fair share of allure.

'It was astonishing the way that Oliver and your parents just clicked,' she remarked, happily reminiscing.

His hands in the pockets of his jeans, Garson strolled into the room and, once again, she was made aware of his size. By anyone's definition he was tall, but he was also well built and firmly muscled. Did he work out in hotel gyms when he travelled? she wondered. He must.

'Like we click,' Garson said.

Anya thought of how they had chatted in the car, of how their tastes had meshed over The Grange, of how, from the start, it had been apparent that they shared the same sense of humour.

'I suppose so,' she agreed.

His blue eyes tangled with hers. 'And we'd click in bed.'

Anya's nerves jumped. A warning bell rang in her head. To be flattered by Garson's interested looks was one thing, to climb between the sheets with him would be another. She recognised that some girls would simply seize the chance, enjoy it, and move on; but for her going to bed involved making a commitment. All right, she did not want to spend the rest of her life alone and craved closeness, yet did she want to make a commitment to him? A commitment which could only mean having an affair.

'Bed?' she repeated uncertainly.

Garson sat down beside her, the mattress dipping beneath his weight. 'Anya,' he said, 'you know that you and I are going to wind up making love.'

With his words, the atmosphere had become charged and heavy. The air seemed to throb.

'I don't know that,' she jabbered.

He smiled a slow, sure, very masculine smile. 'Yes, you do,' he said, and bent his head towards hers.

As Garson tasted the tender curve of her lips, his kiss was soft and almost lazy. Anya curled her fingers tight into her palms. She would not react, she told herself. She must not react. It did not matter that her blood was chasing like quicksilver through her veins or that his tongue had begun a subtle teasing of the outline of her mouth; she refused to be seduced. Yet when he drew back a minute or two later her body cried out for more. Much more.

'Admit it,' Garson murmured.

Lifting her chin, Anya looked defiantly back into his eyes. 'I admit nothing.'

He bent towards her again, but this time when he kissed her his hands slid up beneath her shirt and around her back to deftly unhook her bra. As his fingers spread over the globes of her naked breasts, she gave a strangled gasp. She pulled back, but Garson leant forward, his mouth recapturing hers, and as his tongue thrust between her lips Anya's defiance died. With the erotic blending of their mouths, with the caresses of his hands, he seemed to have touched something inside her which robbed her of any will-power and which demanded her submission.

Unbuttoning her shirt, Garson slid it and her bra from her in one smooth movement and dropped them aside, then he clasped his hands around her upper arms and lowered her gently down and around until she lay full length on the bed. He looked down at her and as his gaze feasted on her breasts, on the smooth honeyed skin, on their taut rose-brown peaks, his eyes smouldered and darkened. Again he caressed her, his thumbs grazing over the rigidity of her nipples and circling the puckered skin of their aureoles. Anya trembled. Desire was surging within her in a heated, sensual tide.

'Garson...' she said, and as if in response to the unspoken plea he lay down beside her.

Taking her into his arms, he kissed her again. At first he kissed her mouth, but in time his kisses moved down, gilding the silken column of her throat and the burgeoning fullness of her breasts. Entwining her fingers into the thick dark hair which grew on top of his head, Anya drew him closer.

Now Garson was kissing her nipples, tasting and gently biting them. Now he was stroking her, his hands languorously exploring the contours of her shoulders, her breasts, the plateau of her belly. Frustration stirred within her. She wanted to stroke him and feel his nakedness. She longed to press her open mouth to his body.

When he pulled back to sit above her, Anya gazed up at him. He must have sensed her need and was going to take off his shirt. Hurry, please hurry, she implored silently.

'You believe me?' Garson asked.

At a loss, she blinked. His manner seemed calm and emotionless, whereas she felt as if she was about to disintegrate into a million swirling pieces.

'Be-believe you?' she stammered. 'About what?'

'That it's our destiny to make love.'

Anya nodded. What else could she do when she was aching to pull him back down onto the bed, when her body hungered for his and for the sexual satisfaction which was so far away and yet tantalisingly near?

When he continued to sit upright, she frowned up at him. 'You were just—just proving a point?' she enquired.

'Not just,' Garson said, 'but yes.'

Icy fingers clutched at her heart. She had, it seemed, been the victim of a deliberate charm offensive.

'Hit 'em hard, hit 'em low—that's the way you operate?' Anya demanded, her anger making her want to raise her voice, to shout at him, but, because Oliver was in the next room, needing to restrict herself to a fierce whisper.

'Pardon me?'

Pushing herself up, she grabbed for her discarded clothes. 'I told you I hadn't made love for two years,' she said as she rapidly hooked on her bra, 'and now—'

'Now you're vulnerable and I'm taking advantage? You don't understand.'

'What I understand is that you are a rat!' Anya declared, and, gathering up her shirt and trousers, she strode onto the landing and ran down the stairs.

'I'll make the coffee,' Garson said, following her down into the living room a moment or two later.

Anya paused in pulling on her shirt to fling him a furious look. 'No, you can bog off!'

Infuriatingly, he smiled. 'Bog off? That's not exactly Shakespeare. But we're going to sit down and talk,' he informed her, in a voice which brooked no argument, 'so we might as well have a coffee. You take milk and one sugar, right?'

'Right,' she snapped.

His disappearance into the kitchen gave Anya time to finish dressing and retrieve a measure of composure. As she thought of how easily Garson had been able to arouse her and how coolly he had switched off, she glowered. It seemed that all he needed to do was look at her and her senses went haywire.

She sank down on the sofa. So how did she fight him? She could not. Becoming his mistress was not something which appealed, nor a situation she would find easy to live with, Anya thought defeatedly, yet the desires of her body left her no choice.

'Are you going to throw this over me?' Garson enquired when he handed her a mug of hot coffee a few minutes later.

She shone him a narrow smile. 'No, though it's what you deserve.' Anya waited until he had sat down beside her, then drew in a breath. 'You've proved—' she groped for the words '—that I can't resist you, so if you want us to have an affair—'

'I don't,' he said.

A pulse beat in her throat. Her nerves screamed. It had not been enough that he had shown how effortlessly he could get her into bed if he so wished—he was now saying he did not want her there. How was that for humiliation? What a kick to her ego! Anya frowned. Yet despite his cool and controlled switch-off Garson had been aroused. The stiffening of his body had made it plain that he desired her.

'No?' she asked uncertainly.

'No, and whilst you might accept such a situation you don't want us to have an affair either.'

Raising the mug to her lips, Anya took a restorative sip of coffee. 'True. I wouldn't feel happy about the example I'd be setting Oliver, nor about what Bert and Kirsten and some of the people in the village might think. And say. Maybe I'm old-fashioned, but the prospect of following in Mrs Collis's footsteps—' she gave a fractured smile '—even in a far more restrained way, doesn't thrill me. But if you aren't interested in an affair,' she continued, perplexed, 'what do you want?'

'I want us to get married.'

There was a long, shocked moment when she gawked at him, then Anya gave a strangled laugh. 'That's a . . . novel idea.'

'But an entirely logical one,' Garson said. 'I'm sick of coming back to an empty apartment to spend much of my free time alone and I have the impression that you're becoming tired of living on your own too. However, if we get married and live together in The Grange, for a start, it means we each have company.'

She looked at him. '"For a start" appears to indicate that you have everything worked out.'

He nodded. 'I do.'

'I should've guessed,' Anya said tautly. 'So this is another proposition you're offering me—like doing up The Grange?'

'You could call it that,' Garson agreed, but he frowned as though he found her interpretation offensive. 'I'd like to bring Oliver more closely into the Deverill family and this way I can do it. Oliver will also benefit from having a man around the place. The child-care manuals would insist that I'd provide a steadying influence, a role model and help make him rounded as a person.'

She flashed him a brittle glance. 'You've been doing your homework.'

'If we get married I'll also look after Oliver financially,' he continued, 'and look after you.'

Anya's backbone stiffened. 'No, thanks; I'm not being bought!'

'I have no intention of buying you,' Garson grated, 'but for you, as my wife, to continue to scrape by on your current earnings when I have more than ample funds wouldn't make sense. My suggestion is that I'd give you an allowance each month, the amount to be agreed.'

'You'd leave it in notes on the dressing-table in the bedroom?' she enquired glacially.

'No, because I'm not buying your sexual favours either. I don't need to buy them.' Garson stretched out a long-fingered hand towards her. 'All I need to do is touch and you'll *give*. Yes?'

Anya flushed. The truth was shaming. 'Yes,' she muttered.

He withdrew his hand. 'So?'

'If I did agree—*if*,' she stressed, 'all I'd accept would be housekeeping money. I wouldn't take any for myself.'

Garson frowned. 'Do you have to be so bloody independent?' he demanded.

'Yes!'

'Done, though if Oliver should need things—'

'Like a clown at his birthday party?' Anya said.

He grinned. 'Clowns, skateboards, private education if you wish it—whatever—then I'd pay. We may not be head over heels in love,' Garson continued, and paused, his expression becoming momentarily brooding, 'but true loves don't present themselves too often. However, we function well together—in *all* spheres.'

At his emphasis of the word his blue eyes met hers, and her heart began to race. Even now, although the mood had become businesslike, Anya was aware of an underlying sexual tension. And so, it seemed, was he.

'I guess,' she said, as nonchalantly as she could.

'You want Oliver to be emotionally secure and so do I,' Garson went on, 'which means I intend our marriage to be for ever.'

'Until death us do part?'

'Amen,' he replied soberly.

Anya fiddled with the end of her plait. 'But suppose, after a couple of years, you met someone else, someone with whom you did fall head over heels in love?'

'It won't happen.'

'How do you know?'

'I know,' Garson said, and his tone was certain. His brow furrowed. 'However, if you should meet someone—'

'Not me,' she cut in.

'So think it over. Now.'

'You want my answer this evening?' Anya protested. Garson nodded. 'I do.'

She took a mouthful of coffee. Whilst there was an undeniable attraction in the idea of forming a family and escaping from the constant anxiety over money—and in sharing Garson's bed, a sneaky voice added—her main consideration was Oliver. She wanted to protect him, provide stability and give him the best chances in life—and Garson's proposition seemed to guarantee all that. The little boy would become part of a family and today she had seen how important that was to him.

'You'd expect me to take Oliver over to see your parents when you're away, or for them to visit here?' Anya enquired.

'Please.'

'And as far as they and everyone else were concerned it'd be a proper marriage?'

'Yes.' Garson fixed her with a level blue gaze. 'As far as I'm concerned, it would be a proper marriage.'

Anya attempted to sort out the tangled skeins of her feelings, the fors and againsts. She was being offered so much and yet... Garson's proposition was *not* a proposal. He might want them to live together as man and wife, but only because it would satisfy certain of his needs and not because he felt unable to live without her. Anya's heart clenched. His suggestion might be logical, yet it seemed too dispassionate, too organised. It did not satisfy her feminine hankering for romance. So assert yourself, an inner voice urged.

'I need more time to consider,' she declared, the light of obstinacy coming into her eyes.

Garson shook his head. 'It's now or never. I want your answer tonight, otherwise we scrap the idea and I get the hell out of your life.'

'Completely?' Anya said, in surprise.

'Completely.' The word was incisive.

'And if I say no to your proposition, what happens?' she enquired.

'Same thing.'

'You'd sell The Grange and the cottages?'

He nodded. 'And I'd never come to Lidden Magnor again.'

Anya flung him an angry look. If he sold up, then her and Oliver's future in the village would be thrown into the melting pot again.

'So it's either your way or no way?' she demanded.

'You got it.'

'You'd deprive Oliver of his grandparents—and them of him?'

Garson crossed a denimmed leg over the other knee and clasped his ankle. 'What do you think?' he asked.

Anya glowered. What she thought was that, whilst Dulcie and Edwin Deverill would be broken-hearted not to see the little boy again, the bottom line was that they would do whatever Garson decreed. She could always try to set up some separate secret arrangement with them, she mused, but his parents were elderly and frail—and might not feel inclined to deceive him.

'You play hardball,' she accused.

'Maybe, yet I usually accomplish what I set out to accomplish,' Garson replied.

Anya believed him. A mental adding up showed that the fors by far outweighed the againsts, so why not stop battling and agree to his proposition? Because the man is steamrollering you, said the voice in her head. Because this isn't how a marriage is supposed to be. As Anya set down her empty mug, she set aside her doubts and misgivings. The essential consideration was Oliver's well-being and the child could only benefit from their alliance.

'My answer is yes,' she said.

Garson smiled. 'Don't worry, everything'll work out fine,' he said, and, moving closer, he pressed his hand against hers, fingertip to fingertip, palm to palm, pressing gently as though making a solemn pact.

'However, I'd like us to be married quietly in a registry office and with no fuss,' Anya went on, determined to claim some rights, 'so that the media don't get to hear about it.'

'I agree. We could honeymoon abroad,' he suggested. 'Perhaps in Mauritius or—'

'No, thanks,' she interrupted.

'You don't want to leave Oliver for too long? OK, though I'm sure he'd be happy with my parents.'

Anya did not doubt that the little boy would be happy with them too, but as she would have been ill at ease exchanging vows in a church, so she would feel awkward with a honeymoon. She winced. The pretence of playing head-over-heels-in-love newly-weds for the benefit of others held scant appeal.

'Then suppose we spend a few days at my apartment in London?' Garson said. 'We could stroll in the parks, go to the theatre—' he lifted a brow '—dine at smart restaurants and sample the sophisticated nightlife.'

Aware that he was feeding her own long-ago phrases back to her, Anya nodded. 'I'd like that.'

For a few minutes they discussed the arrangement of a wedding which he insisted must be as soon as possible and it was agreed that, although her uncle and aunt would probably not be able to fly back for the ceremony, his parents, Bert and Kirsten and her family would be invited. And, of course, Oliver would be the star guest. Having fixed that he would collect her the next morning and they would go to the nearest registry office to set the process in motion, Garson rose to his feet.

'I'd better say goodnight.'

Although Anya immediately jumped up to go with him to the door, she could not stop a sneaky regret. She had been wondering whether now that their relationship was guaranteed he might feel inclined to start making love to her again, only this time he would not stop.

At the door, Garson drew her close and kissed her, long and lingeringly. 'I want to sleep with you very, very much,' he murmured, 'but I'd rather we started off our married life new to each other. Yes?' he asked, in a tone which suggested he was willing to be dissuaded.

Anya hesitated. Whilst she would not be a virgin bride, their restraint would endow the wedding ceremony with a depth, a purity, more meaning. 'Yes,' she agreed, and he kissed her again. 'When we're married, what about us having children?' she enquired as he turned to go.

'There'll be no children.'

'But—' Anya started to protest.

'End of discussion,' Garson said tersely, and left.

CHAPTER SEVEN

ANYA hurtled through the door of the coffee-shop, zig-zagged between the tables and dived into the booth. 'They want twenty boxes of greeting cards, ten of assorted pot-pourri sachets, a dozen flower-trimmed straw hats and six collage pictures,' she reported breathlessly. Her unwieldy bag of samples was dumped onto the bench seat. 'As soon as possible!'

Garson chuckled. 'Although I hate to say it, I told you.'

'OK, but I never truly believed *they'd* be interested in my goods.'

'Why on earth not? It may be a top people's store, but your products are top quality and can compete with the best.' He indicated her cup. 'Would you like another cappuccino?'

They had had coffees together earlier when Garson had been giving her a last-minute pep talk and he had drunk a second while he had read the morning paper and waited.

'No, thanks.'

'And as well as your products being the cream of the crop, their creator's pretty tasty too,' Garson added.

Grinning at him, Anya threaded her fingers into the thickness of her hair, pushing the loose brown curls up into a happy haystack. 'You think so?'

He reached across the table to take hold of her hand. 'I know so. And I've no doubt your tastiness must've helped when you were shooting the guy your sales pitch.'

'But the vital help was you, because it was you who insisted that I should brave their hallowed portals,' she said.

Garson had suggested that when they were honey-mooning at his apartment she should take the opportunity to call into a nearby world-famous department store and show them her dried flower range. Although she had felt doubtful of her chances and more than a little nervous, Anya had made an appointment and, on the spot, had been awarded a healthy order.

'So now, when you go the rounds of your regular customers or approach new outlets, you'll be able to tell them that an élite London store stocks your goods,' he said.

'Thanks to you.' Anya raised his fingers to her lips. 'I kiss your hand in abject worship, oh, master.'

'Uh-uh,' Garson muttered.

'What?'

His blue eyes were slumbrous. 'You've put me in the mood again.'

Anya's heartbeat quickened. They had been married for four days and had spent the first three of them almost continuously in bed. There had been breaks to drink the wine and eat the smoked salmon, mangoes and *crème brûlée* from a hamper of delicacies which Garson had bought and which he'd declared was 'the food of love'— but the breaks had rapidly given way to yet more lovemaking.

'You want something more than your fingers kissed?' she enquired.

His gazed fixed on hers, he nodded. 'I'd also like to indulge in some kissing myself,' he said, the pad of his thumb circling slowly and sensuously in her palm. 'So how's about we grab a cab and head home?'

'Right now?'

'Right now,' Garson said, in a voice which sounded like honey poured over charcoal.

'But I thought we were going to have lunch at a smart restaurant,' Anya demurred.

'We can have dinner or maybe leave eating out until tomorrow.' He rose to his feet. 'Hurry,' he said.

Outside the coffee-shop, the city-centre street was busy. Shoppers thronged the pavement, while cars, taxis and the ubiquitous red double-decker buses sped past on the road.

'Damn!' Garson complained, a few minutes later. 'Every cab we've seen has been occupied.'

Anya smiled. 'Be patient.'

'But I want to make love to you. Now. We're in luck!' he exclaimed suddenly as a black taxi swung into the kerb further down the street and, taking a tighter grip on her hand, he drew her along with him.

As they approached, Anya saw the shadowy en-actment of the fare being paid, then the cab door swung open. A blonde in her mid-thirties stepped out, took a couple of precise steps forward on her stiletto heels and stopped dead.

'Garson. Darling!' she cried, her face lighting up in delight.

He straightened. 'Isobel,' he said carefully.

Her interest firing on all cylinders, Anya looked at the woman. With hair as glossy as mink and discreetly made up, she looked even prettier in real life than she did on the screen. Couture-dressed in a black slim-skirted gros-grain suit which veered close to the body, the television presenter was impossibly stylish and serenely sure of herself. She would not have felt nervous about visiting the department store, Anya thought—though the idea of someone so sophisticated promoting home-made dried flowers seemed rather incongruous.

'Anya, this is Isobel Dewing. Isobel, meet Anya,' Garson said, curtly introducing them.

'Hello there,' the blonde said, and smiled one of her sweet smiles, the kind of smile which Anya found it impossible not to smile back at. 'I believe you were married at the weekend, down in Dorset?'

'That's right,' Anya replied.

How did Isobel know? she wondered. Had Dulcie told her or might Garson have telephoned? She supposed that advising a first wife of the intention to acquire a second was no more than common courtesy, yet the thought of him talking about her—and saying what?—was unsettling.

'I trust the day went off well?' Isobel enquired.

Garson had let go of her hand, and Anya hitched up the slipping strap of her shoulder bag and clung onto the misshapen sample bag which swung against her legs. All the older woman carried was a neat clutch purse.

'It did, thanks,' she replied.

'I'm so pleased—' there was another sweet smile '—and I do hope the two of you will be very happy together.'

Isobel Dewing is *nice*, Anya thought, in despair, then realised that Garson's gaze was moving between the two of them as if he might be comparing them. A dull ache settled behind her ribs. Any comparison was not to her advantage.

'We must be going,' Garson said, and ushered Anya ahead of him into the cab. He turned back to the blonde. 'Goodbye.'

Placing a hand on his arm, Isobel reached up to kiss his cheek. 'Bye, darling. Lovely to see you again,' she said, and swung gracefully away.

She had never met anyone so well groomed before, Anya brooded as the cab plunged into the traffic. There had not been a single crease or a speck of lint on Isobel's suit. She glanced down at the pale green coat dress which she had bought as her going-away outfit. She had considered she was smart, but now...

Anya gave a wry smile. When Garson had carried her into his apartment, he had been in a hurry to undress her and afterwards her clothes had lain on the floor for a while, which explained the odd wrinkle. Her thoughts moved on to Isobel's hair. It was the kind seen in shampoo commercials: shiny, smooth and swinging, with not a strand out of place.

'Isobel is so perfect,' Anya said wistfully, and tugged at a mussed-up curl. 'Perfect hair, perfect clothes—'

'OK, she's a knockout,' Garson rasped. 'But don't make a big thing of it.'

In the silence which followed, Anya turned to look out at the traffic. She had felt jealous when she had imagined how Isobel Dewing must have looked as his bride, but now jealousy made a large, suffocating ball inside her.

Garson put his hand on her knee. 'Anya, the woman is in the past,' he said more gently. 'It's you and me now. Together.' His fingers slid on to her thigh. 'And very soon I shall—'

He spent the rest of the journey describing what he intended to do to her, and in such erotic detail that by the time the elevator delivered them to his fourth-floor apartment Anya's skin was tingling and her heart thumped.

'Do you think this could be the Italian side of you coming out?' she teased as he steered her through to the bedroom and began stripping off her clothes with fevered haste.

Garson paused for a moment to grin. 'That's my excuse for the sexual excesses of the past few days. What's yours?' he enquired.

'Don't have one,' Anya said, and he laughed and kissed her.

Starting on a sensual journey down her body, he mouthed her rigid nipples, kissed the smooth plateau of her stomach, pushed his tongue into the moist tangle of short dark curls at her thighs. At his touch, Anya arched her spine and cried out. He moved up beside her, kissed her again, then rolled her on top of him and slid into her. Closing her eyes, she bit into her lip. Garson was a powerful and exciting lover, yet always mindful of her pleasure.

'That feels so good,' she said, rocking forward above him.

He captured her breasts in his hands. 'How about that?' he muttered, erotically working his hips against hers as he drew one stiffened nipple into his mouth and rolled the other between a thumb and a fingertip.

Anya groaned. 'Wonderful.'

'Open your eyes,' Garson commanded, pulling back. 'Watch me.'

She obeyed, and the sight of his tongue lapping at the stiff, swollen peak of her breast, together with the feel of his feasting mouth, was incredibly arousing. A bolt of emotion sped through her. Her breathing quickened, sweat slicked her skin, the rhythmic rocking of their hips increased.

'God Almighty...Anya,' Garson said hoarsely.

Then he was holding her hips, forcing her closer down on his thighs and himself higher into her. She felt the thrust of him, the heat, the slipperiness—and her body convulsed.

'Again,' he urged. 'Again.'

'I can't,' Anya protested, but her desire was already gathering.

It grew, it built, it exploded. And as she cried out he shuddered and jerked in his own overwhelming climax.

Isobel Dewing means nothing to Garson, Anya assured herself that night as she lay sated and exhausted, with him sleeping beside her. Yes, he had been tense when they had met, but by its nature the introduction of an ex-wife to the new one possessed an in-built tension. She frowned. Even so, she wished the woman had not been so glamorous, so immaculate or so damn pleasant!

'Looks like your business is booming,' someone declared, and Anya turned to see Kirsten coming into the village shop, which served as grocery store-cum-newsagent's-cum-post office.

Smiling, she stuck stamps onto the last of the boxes which she was sending off. 'And how,' she said.

After six weeks, not only had the London store placed a larger, repeat order, but being able to drop its name had already proved to be a magical marketing ploy. It had made her existing customers eager to take her full range and persuaded other gift shops to grant her a trial, which had led to an increase in outlets and increased sales.

'Did you know that Roger Adlam's decided to follow your example and tie the knot?' Kirsten asked as she joined her.

Anya's brows rose in surprise. 'With Fiona?'

'Yes, poor deluded soul.'

Brenda, the gossipy middle-aged shop assistant, leaned across the counter. 'When's the wedding to be?' she enquired.

'In the spring,' Kirsten informed her.

As the two women launched into a discussion of possible hotels for the reception, guests, what kind of dress Fiona might choose, et cetera, Anya remembered how the young farmer had appeared at her cottage door and attempted to restart their non-existent relationship. Not wishing to embarrass him, she had kept quiet about his visit and now whenever they met Roger was amiable, if a little wary. However, his ditching of Fiona must have been speedily rescinded for only days after his visit she had seen the couple together again, arm in arm.

'Would you like a lift home?' Anya asked, when there was a break in the conversation.

'Please,' Kirsten said, and bought her groceries. 'The thatching of the cottages is going great guns,' she commented as they drove back through the village.

'Yes, the men should be finished next week if it stays dry.' Anya looked out at the late September sunshine. 'This far, we've been amazingly lucky with the weather.'

'And as soon as the thatching's complete Bert moves into your cottage while his is renovated?'

'That's right; then he returns home and mine gets the treatment. My increased trade means that the barn's bursting at the seams,' she continued, drawing the Volkswagen to a halt outside Kirsten's house. 'Garson and I were talking about it when he phoned last night and he suggested that I could use my cottage as extra work space.'

'Good idea,' Kirsten said, and grinned. 'Your gorgeous hunk's still hoping to make it home today?'

Anya nodded. 'He had a meeting this morning, but he should be leaving his office around now. He'll be here for a week.'

'I thought Garson's travelling meant he wouldn't be able to visit too often, but he's been here for a long weekend every other weekend since you were married and it's not that long ago since he took a week off for your honeymoon.'

Anya's hazel eyes sparkled. 'Well, he's managed another one.'

'And made his young bride brim with happiness,' Kirsten declared. Gathering up her bags of shopping, she climbed from the car. 'I'm free to babysit if the two of you fancy a couple of evenings out.'

'Thanks, we may, but I'll let you know.'

She *was* happy, Anya thought when, after waving to the thatchers and greeting Bert, who was pruning apple trees, she let herself into The Grange a short while later. All the doubts she had suffered when Garson had put forward his proposition had disappeared. All her resentment at being forced into a decision, then and there, had gone. Their wedding day, which she had secretly dreaded, had been relaxed and their honeymoon had been . . . bliss.

Walking into the kitchen, Anya hugged her arms around herself and smiled. She seemed to be forever smiling these days. Garson was so fond and considerate and easy to be with that, most of the time, she forgot theirs was an arranged marriage. And she felt sure that no one else suspected.

Anya's smile spread. What people probably *did* suspect, what must be difficult to ignore, was the sexual current which sizzled between them. How her husband seemed to constantly need to touch her. How, as if drawn by a magnet, she would veer close to him. How they exchanged glances which smouldered with promised acts of passion. And after those acts of passion and when Garson had left she could often taste him on her fingers and smell him in her hair. And she would daydream.

Opening a cupboard, Anya took out packets of sugar and flour. There was no need to daydream now, for soon

Garson would be here and tonight he would take her to heaven again. But before he arrived there was baking to be done.

An hour later, when she heard the blare of the Maserati's horn, Anya abandoned the mixing bowl she had been washing and hurriedly dried her hands. As she went outside, she saw Garson walking towards her across the yard. He had shed his jacket and was refixing the sleeves of his white shirt, which were rolled halfway up his forearms—tanned, muscled forearms. As he drew nearer, she felt her body start to react to his proximity. Her skin prickled, her breasts tightened, her nervous system moved into overdrive.

Anya swallowed in a breath. It was all she could do not to throw herself at him and start tearing off his clothes.

'Hello, you're early,' she said, trying hard to sound casual. 'Did you have a good journey?'

'Yes, the motorways were quiet so I was able to put my foot down,' Garson replied, but the way he looked at her made it seem as though he was saying one thing out loud and giving her another, more intimate message with his eyes. He reached out to pull her into his arms. 'I've missed you so much,' he said, and his mouth covered hers.

'Ditto,' Anya said breathlessly, when he drew back.

Garson studied her with anxious eyes. 'You're feeling all right?'

Two Sundays ago and after eating what must have been a rogue bad prawn when they had dined out, Anya had suffered a dose of food poisoning and been sick. She had been ill again on the Monday when he had left, though by the next day she had fully recovered.

She smiled at his concern. 'I told you I was fine on the phone. I've told you endless times.'

'I don't like you to be ill,' Garson protested, and kissed her again. 'I've got quite a load,' he said, indicating the car. 'Could you give me a hand?'

'Sure.'

When he opened the boot Anya saw his suitcase, bulging briefcase, laptop computer and half a dozen or so exclusive-looking stiff white carrier bags. The briefcase and computer indicated that he would be doing some work while he was here—as she intended to work on her handicrafts too—but did the bags mean he had been treating himself?

'You've been buying new clothes?' Anya enquired.

Garson grinned. 'Lots.'

He handed her the bags, loaded himself up with the heavier items, and waited for her to lead the way. Going upstairs, Anya crossed the landing and went into the master bedroom, which looked out across the meadows at the rear of the house. Decorated in cream—pale cream walls, pale cream lacquered built-in wardrobes and dressing-table, a thick-pile cream carpet—the room was tranquil, though deep pink and chartreuse striped moiré damask curtains and a pink velvet-upholstered chaise longue added a vibrancy. But since his visit a fortnight ago there had been a change, one which she had kept secret.

'What do you think?' Anya enquired, turning to smile back at him as he followed her into the room.

Garson looked at the four-poster in surprise, laughed and put down his cargo. 'I think it's fantastic. When did it arrive?'

Although the bed had been ordered the day after it had been agreed that they would marry—he had insisted that a four-poster was essential—the one they had chosen was handmade so had a lengthy delivery date. January had been quoted.

'Last Monday,' she said, and followed his gaze.

Cream calico frills frothed like thistledown around the top framework of the bed, the four posts were smoothly twisted, the rosewood head and footboards gleamed. The same calico as the frills covered four plump pillows and the coverlet consisted of a vast sheet of deep rose silk, overlaid with heavy cream lace.

'Have you been sleeping in it?' Garson enquired.

Anya shook her head. 'I had the other bed put into the spare room and I slept there.'

'You wanted to wait until we—' his voice took on a throaty timbre '—were together?'

'It seemed . . . appropriate,' she replied, and an almost palpable flare of incandescence passed between them.

'My purchases are appropriate too,' Garson said, and, up-ending two of the white bags, he tipped their contents out onto the bed. 'For you.'

Cosseted amongst sheets of tissue paper, Anya found a pale lilac chiffon negligée trimmed with deeper lilac lace and a matching lilac teddy. A quivering sensation went down her spine. The teddy was cut revealingly low at the bodice and high at the hips.

'French?' she enquired, stroking the lace.

'That's what was specified.' Garson's eyes held hers. 'Remember?'

Anya smiled. 'I remember.'

He took hold of the remaining bags and emptied out their contents. 'These are for you too.'

Again thickets of tissue paper had to be unwrapped, yet as pretty-coloured sets of silk bras and briefs, lacy underslips, a flowered basque and a topaz-coloured nightgown were revealed Anya's smile died. Because she no longer needed to pay for basics such as food, she was in the unusual position of having money to spend on herself, and so she had begun to restock her wardrobe.

As well as the coat dress, she had bought a navy reefer jacket, a pencil-slim cream skirt and a couple of silky jewel-coloured shirts, but her underclothes had yet to be replaced.

Anya frowned down. Whilst Garson's purchase of the negligée and teddy could be construed as a joke, she did not find the idea of him buying the other items quite so amusing. Ever since they had met Isobel Dewing, thoughts of the woman had been scratching around at the back of her mind, and now it struck her that this was precisely the kind of luxury designer lingerie which she would wear.

Garson had appeared to compare them at the time of the meeting, but had he been comparing them ever since? As Anya visualised her well-worn underwear, her spirits slumped. In that department there was no comparison. He had not criticised, yet could he have decided to upgrade her? Might he have been in the habit of buying Isobel's lingerie himself and have even chosen identical garments? Anya squirmed. The idea filled her with distaste.

'You bought everything?' she enquired. 'You didn't send your secretary?'

Garson looked indignant. 'I shopped myself,' he said, and his lips curved in a sudden grin. 'But I've never bought stuff like this before and I have to confess that I needed to pluck up my courage before I approached the salesgirl.'

He might not have previously purchased lingerie, but he could know which store Isobel patronised and have visited the same one, Anya brooded. She did not relish that idea either.

'Everything's your size,' he said.

'I know,' she muttered.

'You don't like what I've chosen?'

'I like it very much,' Anya replied distractedly.

'Give me strength!' Garson rasped, all of a sudden. 'Anya, this is not charity and I'm not trying to encroach on your precious independence.' Spreading two hands around her waist, he pulled her impatiently against him. 'You're a beautiful young woman with beautiful silky skin which cries out for beautiful silky clothes to be worn next to it, and I would deem it a privilege if you would allow me—your husband, dammit!—to give you this underwear.' He glared furiously down at her. 'Is that permissible?'

Anya smiled up into his angry eyes. She was being foolish. Garson's only thought when he had bought the lingerie had been *her*—spoiling her, wanting her to feel good, wanting her to look good. Isobel Dewing had not featured in his reckoning. As he had said, the woman was long gone, a back number, history.

'It's not just permissible, everything is most acceptable,' she said, and reached up to kiss him. 'Thank you.'

Placated, he tilted his head. 'Would it also be permissible for you to abandon your tights and indulge my male fantasies by wearing stockings instead?' Reaching in amongst the clouds of tissue paper, he extracted a frilly black suspender belt and dangled it from one finger. 'The whole ensemble is not only far sexier, but it means that when I'm away I'll be able to imagine your long legs striding around in black nylon stockings with that temptingly exposed strip of pale golden thigh.'

Anya grinned. 'It'll turn you on?'

'*You* turn me on. Whatever you're wearing and if you're wearing nothing at all. Just you,' Garson told her gravely, and jettisoned the suspender belt. 'Hair first,' he said, and, reaching behind her head, he lifted her plait over her shoulder.

'I have to pick Oliver up at three,' she protested as he started to take off the band.

Turning his wrist, he glanced at his watch. 'So we have an hour.' The tip of his tongue protruding out between his lips in concentration, Garson unfastened her hair then swung it loose and lush around her shoulders. 'You're supposed to wear the teddy and the negligée, but we'll leave that for next time,' he murmured, and started unbuttoning her blouse.

For a moment Anya hesitated, filled with a vague sense of rancour that he should take it for granted that she should want to make love within minutes of him arriving home and that she was being used for his sexual pleasure, but when Garson bent his head and kissed her her thoughts wavered and changed. She was not being used; the pleasure was mutual. She *did* want to make love. Now. Every pore, every cell of her yearned for him.

Her fingers went to her blouse and together they undressed her and, next, together they undressed him. When they faced each other, Anya swallowed. Although on honeymoon she had got to know his body—every freckle, every mole, every scar—each time she saw Garson naked she marvelled at his male beauty.

Travelling the world, he caught sufficient sunshine to maintain a tan, which meant his skin was golden. He also had a disciplined exercise routine which, when he was with her, included a daily run through the village, so his torso was firm-muscled, his thighs strong, his legs lithe and powerful.

As she gazed up at him, he raised a hand and ran it slowly down from her shoulder, grazing the rounded sideswell of her breast, travelling around the inward curve of her waist to caress her hips. Anya drew in a breath. Now his fingers were amongst the dark pubic curls and as he sought and gently probed the moistening secret valley a whimper sounded in her throat.

Sweeping the lingerie and paper aside, Garson threw back the coverlet and drew her down with him onto the four-poster.

'Satin sheets and your hair is like satin,' he murmured and, buttressing himself up on one elbow, he spread out the polished mane until it streamed in lambent strands of russet, sable and copper across the pillow.

'Satisfied?' Anya enquired, smiling into his eyes as he lay back.

'Not yet, but I will be. We both will be,' Garson declared, and he kissed her.

Mouth pressed to heated mouth and limbs entwined, they lay there until, once again, his hand moved down, caressing and touching her on shoulder, breast, stomach and hip, as if he needed to relearn her body—the body which he had known so intimately just two weeks before. Lowering his dark head, he enclosed his mouth around her nipple and as he pulled sharply on the tight-furled bud Anya arched her back and strained against him.

'When I'm away I can't stop thinking about how you feel beneath me, how it feels when I'm inside you. It drives me insane,' Garson muttered, and when he raised his head the hunger she saw in his eyes was so intense it felt like a penetration.

Again he tasted the tender points of her breasts, then he traced a line of darting kisses over the flat plane of her stomach and down to her thighs. As she felt the pressure of his mouth, the flick of his tongue, a heat rolled over her—a raging heat which glossed her brow and flushed her skin. She lifted her hips, needing him, needing more.

'My lusty lady,' Garson murmured.

He parted the glistening wings of her sex and tasted the essence of her, and Anya cried out. She had never realised how wild, how erotic, how *obsessive* lovemaking could be, she thought as she struggled to control the climax which was building inside her. Garson touched her again with his tongue, and abruptly her desire was beating at her, bending her, howling inside her until, in one violent, surging moment, she could no longer forestall the inevitable explosion. Anya shuddered convulsively.

'Not more multiple orgasms?' he enquired.

Smiling, she laid her head against his shoulder. 'Seems so.'

Garson kissed her and caressed her until he had aroused her again. He drew her close and as she felt the hardness of him against her thighs Anya was filled with a need to kiss him. In their passion she had discovered the joy of sexual abandonment and she slid down his body to curl her fingers around his pulsing manhood and press her lips to its tip.

Garson groaned. He submitted to the pleasuring for a few intense moments, then drew her up, twisted her beneath him and slid into her. Arching his long body over her, he held himself still so that she felt the strength of him throbbing, hard and fierce, within her. Anya lifted her pelvis and, recognising her need, he started to move.

Once again she felt a climax building. His thrusts quickened and deepened, and her climax came closer, closer until it was engulfing and sucking her in. As her fingernails raked at the rolling muscles of his back, Anya gave herself up to the exquisite torture. He moved again, and a searing white light exploded behind her closed eyelids and, as she cried out, her whole body seemed to open and burst and melt over his hardness.

*   *   *

Anya looked at the clock. It was barely seven and the alarm had still to ring. She smiled. After a week when she and Garson had repeatedly made love—often during the day, always at bedtime and sometimes waking to reach for each other in the middle of the night—she ought to have been exhausted, but instead she thrived. Turning her head, she gazed at the man who lay sleeping on the pillow beside her. With his dark hair fallen over his brow and his eyes closed, he looked touchingly rumpled and defenceless. And perhaps a bit like Oliver.

She felt a contraction of her throat. Once she had regarded Garson as yet another dose of bad luck, but meeting him had turned out to be the greatest good fortune. He might not have been named after a knight, but in marrying her he had effectively galloped up on a white charger and rescued the beleaguered damsel from all the perils.

As she gazed at him, his eyelids slowly lifted and he smiled. 'Good morning,' Garson murmured and, rolling closer, he stretched a muscled leg over hers.

As Anya felt the pressure of his thighs, her heartbeat broke into a chaotic rhythm. 'Again?' she protested, trying to sound jokey though desire was already nipping within her.

'You should know by now what happens when I wake up beside you,' he said, and his arm came around her. 'And I think we might just have time for—' The yowling siren of a toy police car sounded in Oliver's room. 'We don't.'

She inched closer. 'When Oliver knocks on the door and asks if he can come in—'

'Which we decided he must, because we don't want to be caught *in flagrante delicto*,' Garson inserted.

'—one of us could say that the other one's sleeping.'

'And send him away? Shame on you,' he chided, grinning, but a moment later he sobered. 'No. Having to share you is a new experience and I don't want him to regard me as an intruder and feel rejected.'

A smile broke out on her face. 'I can't see that happening,' Anya replied as she thought of how Oliver climbed all over him, demanded to be carried on his shoulders, insisted that he must play with the incessantly blaring police car—a gift which Garson had brought back from an American trip and almost instantly regretted. 'But you're the boss.'

Half an hour later, when they were having breakfast, Oliver suddenly put down the spoon with which he had been shovelling muesli into his mouth and frowned across at Garson.

'Henry Collis says you're not my uncle; he says you're my stepfather,' he told him.

'I'm both,' Garson replied. 'More or less.'

The little boy ate another spoonful of muesli. 'So instead of Uncle Garson I could call you Daddy?'

Garson gave a smile of pure delight. 'I guess,' he said, glancing at Anya, who smiled back. 'If you want to.'

'I want to,' Oliver said seriously, then added, 'And you can call me son.'

'That's very kind. As I'll be gone when you come home, would you like me to drive you to school this morning—son?' he enquired.

The child beamed. 'Yes, please. I shall tell Henry Collis that I have a daddy and two mummies,' he declared.

'You will?' Anya said.

Oliver nodded. 'This morning.'

'And yah boo to you, Henry,' Garson muttered, under his breath.

When they had departed, Anya stacked the dishwasher and took out the ironing board. Because Garson had insisted that it was too much to expect her to produce her handicrafts and care for a house the size of The Grange, they had employed a local girl who came in to clean twice a week, but this was not one of her days. She plugged in the iron. Garson was leaving for London in an hour, and before he left some of his shirts needed to be pressed. He had said he would do them himself, but she wanted to help.

Switching on the radio, Anya tuned into a station which played almost non-stop pop music. As she ironed, her foot began to tap. She smiled, recalling Garson's pleasure when Oliver had asked if he could call him Daddy. He was so fond of the little boy, so why had he vetoed the idea of them having children? she wondered. It did not make sense.

Someday she would persuade him otherwise, Anya decided, though not yet. As his 'no children' command had implied the expectation that she would take the necessary precautions she had gone along to the doctor's surgery and obtained a prescription for the Pill. She would continue to take it for a year maybe, but then she would talk to Garson and...

The next record was a reggae number and, standing back from the ironing board, Anya raised her arms and started to click her fingers. 'Oh, yeah, oh, yeah,' she sang, jiggling her hips in her slim-fitting skirt. When the reggae was replaced by rock, she danced on, her body swaying rhythmically from side to side.

At last the music ended and as the disc jockey started to talk about changing the mood Anya began to iron again. She had got carried away and time was passing.

'As spectator sports go, you dancing has to be one of the greatest,' Garson said, from the doorway.

Startled, she spun round. 'You've been watching me?'

He nodded. 'And I think you're far sexier than your sister.' As the strains of a slow, smoochy number came over the air, he walked across the kitchen to draw her out from behind the ironing board. 'Instead of dancing by yourself, how about dancing with me?'

Pressing his palm into the small of her back, Garson held her close. Anya's pulse rate accelerated. She was fitted against him, and as they started to dance—not moving far, more or less swaying on the spot—the matching of their bodies at chest, waist and groin seemed searingly erotic.

'When will you be here again?' she asked.

'Not for a while.' Garson paused. 'I reckon in about six weeks.'

Anya pulled back. 'Six weeks?' she said, in dismay.

She had believed that the frequency of his visits indicated Garson's urgent need to be with her, and yet, whilst she accepted that his business demanded much of his attention, such a long absence would appear to indicate that his need was not *that* great.

'I want to do some restructuring of my companies and that involves an extensive amount of travelling,' Garson explained, and his arms encircled her. They danced again and his hands began to roam over the contours of her bottom. 'I seem to remember that the Puritans used to rage against the waltz as the devil's own invention,' he muttered and, cupping her buttocks, he pulled her against his thighs.

As she felt the thrust of his arousal, her nerves tingled. Their slow dancing had created the same need within him as it was creating within her. Anya reached up to kiss him and as their mouths locked Garson drew up her skirt. Sliding his hands beneath it, he stroked up over her black lace-topped stockings to caress her naked thighs.

'Pure silk,' he murmured, against her mouth, and a long finger travelled around to gently probe the frilled lace of her panties.

Anya quivered. No matter how often Garson chose to visit her, or how seldom, she would never be able to resist him.

'Let's go to bed,' she said.

Garson smiled down. 'You wanton hussy,' he said.

Whether it was because he would be gone for a long time, or due to the imminence of his departure, she did not know, but their lovemaking was more sensual and hungrier than ever. As they flung off their clothes, his mouth went to her breasts, her thighs, while, at the same time, his hands stroked compulsively over her body. Complaining that this time it was he who could not wait, Garson entered her—though she was ready, so ready—and when it came the release was volcanic.

They lay together for a while as they recovered, but then, belatedly, the remainder of his shirts were ironed, his case was packed and they walked out to his car.

'I shall suffer severe withdrawal symptoms,' Garson said, when he had kissed her goodbye.

Anya gave a stiff smile. 'Me too.'

His arms remained around her. 'I must go,' he said, as if fighting an urge to stay.

There was the sudden crunch of footsteps on the gravel and, when they turned, they saw Bert coming around the corner of the barn, pushing a wheelbarrow.

The old man grinned at the tableau they presented. 'Just off?' he said to Garson. 'Perhaps the next time you're down we could pay that visit to the races?'

Although Garson replied with a smile, Anya sensed his silent groan. At their wedding reception, Bert had cornered him and made a point of saying again how he much enjoyed attending race meetings, but, alas, and alack, could rarely manage it. Feeling pressurised, Garson had suggested that perhaps one day he could take him. It had been a casual offer, yet ever since the old man had been issuing constant reminders and trying to pin him down.

'If you give Anya a copy of the meetings calendar, I'll select a date when I telephone and she can see if it suits you,' Garson said.

'Any date'll suit me,' Bert assured him, and trundled contentedly off.

Taking Anya back into his arms, Garson kissed her again and then, muttering that he *must* go, he wrenched himself away and climbed into the car.

'Until next time, my love,' he said, and the engine fired, there was a swish of tyres, and the Maserati sped away.

Although Anya waved a smiling goodbye, as she returned indoors her heart was heavy. After they had made love earlier she had cried, overwhelmed by the intensity of her feelings, and in that moment—an avalanche moment—she had realised that she loved Garson. There had been no need to think about it; she had known.

Though she should have known earlier, Anya brooded, for, in retrospect, she felt sure that she would never have agreed to marry him—even under pressure—unless she had loved him. And wasn't that why, when Garson had suggested that she might meet someone else and fall for them, she had been so certain when she had said 'Not me'?

Anya sat down at the kitchen table. Yet, although he called her 'my love' and gave her involuntary kisses the way lovers did, Garson did not love *her*. He had made that brutally plain when he had put forward his proposition. He might miss her and be driven insane by desire, yet he had never said 'I love you', not even in the heat of their lovemaking. She sank her head in her hands. She supposed she should be grateful that he did not lie, yet she almost felt she would prefer it if he did attempt to deceive her with expressions of love.

A hollowness formed inside her. Not so long ago, their marriage had seemed like immense good fortune, but now the prospect of spending the rest of her life loving Garson when he did not love her had turned it into a gilded trap.

CHAPTER EIGHT

'I WAS saying to my neighbour, Mollie—a leading light in the dramatic society, was Mollie, though that must be, ooh, fifteen years ago. Doesn't time fly?' The old lady paused, having lost her thread, then picked it up again. 'I was saying to Mollie that it was a while since I last saw your husband jogging through the village.'

'He's been away on business and only arrived back last night,' Anya explained.

She was sitting in the foyer at the doctor's surgery waiting for her number to light up on the board and the old lady, whom she knew by sight, had swooped down as if she were a long-lost friend and begun to chat. Anya frowned at the board. When Garson had left, she had been filled with the rosy hope that he would be stricken with such desperate *need* for her that he would abandon his restructuring and rush home, at least for a weekend, yet she had hoped in vain. And, as if to demonstrate how foolishly cock-eyed her hopes were, he had been absent for not just six weeks but for eight.

'Bert Cox was telling me how he and your husband have it planned to go to the races,' the old lady gossiped on.

'They're there this afternoon,' Anya told her.

'Then I hope Bert keeps well wrapped up. It might be sunny, but there's a wintry nip to the air and us senior citizens feel it.' The old lady drew her coat collar up around her neck. 'I'm here with a chill. Prone to chills, I am. Last year I had one which developed into influenza, a real bad bout it was and—'

160

For a while Anya kept pace with the jeremiad of aches and pains which followed, but inevitably her thoughts strayed—back to Garson. Time was said to heal, and it did. After spending what had seemed like interminable days and nights agonising over the hopelessness of falling in love with a man who did not love her, she had finally come to terms with it.

She had been aware of his feelings from the start, so had no grounds for complaint. Indeed, by agreeing to his proposition she could be said to have made her own fate. And, even if Garson was not in love with her, he did make the most wonderful love *to* her, seemed to care about her and had vowed to be loyal. She could live with that.

Anya lowered her head. All right, maybe her hurt was not so much healed as covered over with sticking plaster, but she could cope. Besides, there was always a chance that, given time, Garson's desire might deepen into love. Her lips curved as she recalled the passionate and tender reunion which they had shared last night. Surely the chance had to be strong?

'Isn't that your appointment, dear?' the old lady enquired, tugging at her sleeve.

Startled, Anya glanced up at the board. 'Oh, yes; thank you.'

Oliver gave a noisy sigh. 'Mummy, you're not listening.'

Anya paused in slicing mushrooms for the casserole which they would be having for dinner. 'Sorry?' she enquired blankly.

'I said that the clock says it's five o'clock and they're not home. You told me they would be home and—' The little boy broke off to listen to the sound of a vehicle drawing onto the yard. 'They're here!' he cried, and sped out of the kitchen.

As he rushed to open the front door, Anya smiled. She had been preoccupied because, after having only just worked through and settled the matter of her unrequited love in her mind, another issue had presented itself. She placed a hand on her stomach. The fact that there was a new life growing inside her.

However, this did not trouble her half as much. Garson might have been against them having a family, but she was convinced that once he got used to the idea he would be pleased. No, she corrected herself, delighted. Garson liked children. He not only had time for Oliver, but also for the friends who came to play with the little boy. He would be a fond and interested father.

Anya tipped the mushrooms into a bowl. Although her pregnancy was totally unexpected and rather soon, it delighted her too. It would be good for Oliver to grow up with a companion, but—the crux—she wanted to bear Garson's child. A primal need surged. She wanted to bear the child of the man she loved. It would be the ultimate commitment.

'Grandad Bert betted on the horses and he's won lots and lots of money!' Oliver informed her, scampering back into the kitchen a minute or two later.

The old man and Garson followed. Fugitives from the dark November evening, their faces glowed and they brought a breath of cold outdoors air in with them.

'Congratulations,' Anya said, and her gaze swung to Garson. As his eyes met hers in a silent smiling greeting, her heart fluttered. 'Did you win anything?'

He shrugged out of his brown sheepskin jacket. 'Not a cent,' he replied, arching mock-soulful brows.

'You will the next time,' Bert declared, taking it for granted that there would be another day out at the races. He looked at Anya. 'I was thinking that if a certain young gentleman and I walked up to the shop just now I could buy him a treat.'

'A treat for me?' Oliver asked, his eyes stretching into wide, pleased circles.

'That's very kind,' she said.

'It was very kind of your husband to take me to the races,' the old man responded.

Garson grinned. 'I enjoyed it.'

Shepherding Oliver out to the cloakroom, Anya zipped an anorak over his sweater and trousers, added bobble hat and gloves and, as the child speculated excitedly on what his treat might be, sent him off with his companion.

'Did you really enjoy yourself?' she asked, when she returned to the kitchen.

Garson placed a hand on either side of her head and drew her close. 'Yes, though I would far rather've spent the afternoon with you,' he said, and kissed her with a searching, open-mouthed kiss. 'Later,' he murmured, stepping back.

Anya felt the stirrings of that divine ache. 'Later,' she agreed.

'Would you like a glass of wine?' he enquired.

Although they usually had a drink before dinner, Anya hesitated. The doctor had not listed any dos and don'ts of pregnancy—those would come later when she visited the prenatal clinic—but she recollected reading a recommendation to go steady on alcohol.

'I'd better not,' she said.

Garson gave her a quizzical look. 'Why better not?'

She had intended to break the news to him later that evening, after Oliver had gone to bed and when they were sitting quietly alone, but all of a sudden she could not wait. All of a sudden, she needed to tell him *now*.

A smile danced unbidden around the edge of her mouth. 'Because I'm going to have a baby.'

Garson stared, wide-eyed, and raised a bewildered hand to his head. He looked so much a picture of stupefied astonishment that it was comical, and Anya almost laughed.

'A baby?' he repeated. 'Are you sure?'

'Positive; the doctor confirmed it today. I know it's a heck of a shock; it was for me too,' she said, when he continued to stare at her, 'but although I made a point of always taking the Pill, as instructed—'

'You were on the Pill?'

Puzzled, she looked at him. Why did he ask that? Garson had not used any protection himself, so he must have realised. Though perhaps he thought she had been using some form of internal contraception.

'Yes, but when I was sick with the food poisoning apparently that nullified the effect,' Anya explained. 'And the doctor reckons we must both be very fertile. I know you didn't want us to have children—not yet, anyway—and I was willing to abide by that, but now—'

'It can't be mine,' Garson said.

For a moment his words hung suspended in silence, then they hit her like a hand grenade, exploding in her face and stunning, blinding, shattering. Anya reeled back. As his brother had repudiated her sister's unborn child, so Garson was now repudiating hers!

Numb and incredulous, she gazed at him, until suddenly a great tide of emotion swept her up and she was running from the room, snatching her car keys from the hall table, flinging herself out through the front door and into the battered Volkswagen. As tears blurred her vision, she jammed the gear stick into gear.

'Anya!' she heard Garson call from behind, and a blurry glance in the rear-view mirror showed him appearing out of the house.

'You bastard!' she said, in a voice which ended in a sob.

Anya skidded off the gravel and out onto the lane. The steering wheel was yanked to the left. She had no idea where she was going and she did not care. She blinked furiously against hot tears. The only thing she knew was that she had to get away.

As she drove down the lane, leaving the village behind, it occurred to her that Garson would make chase in the Maserati, and have no difficulty in catching up. She pressed down on the accelerator pedal as far as it would go and for a mile—or was it two, or three?—kept glancing in the mirror. But she saw no yellow beam of following headlights, just jet-black night.

What was she doing? Anya wondered, all of a sudden. Tearful and distracted and in a state of high agitation, she ought not to be careering recklessly along the lanes at full tilt in the dark like this. She was a danger to other road users and to herself. To her baby! She reduced her speed and as she reached a wide grass verge where New Agers parked their caravans in the summer she bumped onto it. Switching off the engine, Anya looped her arms over the steering wheel and bowed her head.

It couldn't be his child, Garson had said, but whose child did he think it was? She gave a hiccuping, slightly hysterical laugh. She had no idea. Though by now he would have come to his senses and acknowledged that he must be the father. He would have recognised that her desire for him was all-exclusive and there was not the remotest chance of her fancying another man. His denial had been a knee-jerk reaction.

Haphazardly, she wiped at her wet cheeks. Yet, be it knee-jerk or not, Garson had *had* that reaction, which meant that, whilst he had been willing to marry her and lusted after her body, at heart he did not trust her and never had. Tears stung anew. She had thought he cared—earlier today she had even believed there was a chance he might fall in love with her!—but love and caring were based on trust.

Raising her head, Anya listened to the silence. Garson might have followed her out of the house, but no low, gleaming Maserati had come roaring along the lane in anxious pursuit. Why not? Because his caring had been a pretence. She had also been pretending—to herself, she thought wretchedly. She had pretended that their arranged marriage was acceptable, but it was not, never had been and never would be.

Fumbling in the pocket of her jeans for a paper tissue, Anya blew her nose. By marrying her and not loving her, Garson had gouged out her heart, and in spurning her this evening he had trampled on it. He had also taken a chunk of her soul. A large chunk. An irretrievable chunk. The tissue was stuffed away. She loathed the man, she thought furiously. And she loved him. Anya gave a wild snort of self-derision. Contrary though it might be, it seemed perfectly possible to do both!

She turned the key in the ignition. Her flight from the house had also been a knee-jerk reaction—the instinctive fleeing from an attacker—but she needed to confront him. She would go back and tell Garson that the charade must end and she wanted a divorce.

An aching sadness filled her. Oliver was destined to be hurt by their break-up, but she could see no alternative. To continue to live with Garson would be a daily catastrophe for her heart and mind. Though, of course, Anya thought grimly, as by becoming pregnant she had committed the unconscionable sin of ignoring one of his diktats, he might have already finalised his plans to divorce *her*.

A few minutes later, when she drew up outside the front of The Grange, Anya's gaze circled around the shadows. The Maserati was no longer in the yard. Did that mean Garson had made chase, she wondered, and taken a wrong turning? Or, more prosaically, could he have simply put the car away in the garage? After all, as she had dashed out wearing only sweatshirt and jeans, and taking no money, he would have realised she was bound to return before too long.

Anya locked the Volkswagen and walked in through the evening cold. 'I'm back,' she called stiffly.

At her words Oliver bounded out from the drawing room, carrying a box of Lego building bricks. 'Look what Grandad Bert bought me,' he said.

She dredged up a smile. 'Very nice.'

'*And* I've got sweets. Come and see,' he said, and took hold of her hand.

As the little boy drew her along towards the drawing room Anya's nerves tightened like piano wire, but when they entered the only person there was Bert. His coat discarded, he was sitting on the sofa fitting pieces of Lego together into what looked like a lopsided attempt at a plane.

'Hello,' he said cheerfully.

Anya nodded a greeting and hesitated, aware that some kind of explanation for her absence was required. 'Garson and I had an argument,' she said awkwardly, perching herself on the arm of a chair.

'My daddy's not here,' Oliver informed her.

'Oh.' She spoke to Bert. 'Was he here when you came back from the shop?'

'For a minute or two,' the old man replied.

'And he went after me?'

'No, he's gone to London.'

'London?' Anya echoed, in surprise. 'To his apartment?'

Bert shook his head. 'He's gone to see Isobel Dewing.'

'Would you like a sweet, Mummy?' Oliver asked, thrusting a large bag of butterscotch under her nose.

'No, thanks. Isobel?' she demanded.

'Garson said something about if she wasn't at her house he'd need to try the television studios. He seemed a bit worked up.' Bert rose and pulled on his coat. 'He asked me if I'd stay with Oliver until you came back and now that you are back I'll be off home and get myself a bite to eat before I make tracks for the pub.' He bent to pat her hand. 'Don't worry; every marriage has its ups and downs.' The old man winked. 'And think of all the fun the two of you are going to have kissing and making up.'

Anya's reply was a tight smile.

Fortunately Oliver was too absorbed with his building bricks to notice her distraction as they had dinner—scrambled eggs; it was too late to cook the casserole—and then as she bathed him and put him to bed. And he took it for granted that Garson would be back from London by the morning.

Later, as Anya sat in the drawing room leafing unseeingly through a magazine, she frowned. She did not share the child's belief. Garson would be forced to return in order for them to sort things out, but she doubted it would be tonight. A layer of ice settled around her heart. In the moment of crisis, his response had not been to chase after her, but to head off to find his ex-wife.

Anya pushed the magazine aside. Garson's need for Isobel Dewing's shoulder to cry on could only lead to one inescapable conclusion: he still loved the woman. Thinking back, he had made several remarks which could be interpreted as early warning signals, though she had failed to notice their significance at the time.

For example, he had commented on how his travelling made it difficult to make relationships, but, still carrying a torch for Isobel, he would not have tried to make them, nor have wanted to. Until, of course, Ms Prescott had happened onto the scene offering the so convenient package deal of a comfortably furnished house, home cooking and unlimited sex on tap!

Garson had also spoken of true loves not presenting themselves too often, Anya remembered, which could now be seen to mean that he had already found his one and only. And what about his steel-clad certainty, when putting forward the marriage proposition, that he would never fall in love with anyone else? She had been referring to the future, but he had been able to give that guarantee because he was in love and would be for ever in love; with Isobel. Anya gave a bleak smile. Now she understood Garson's reluctance to talk about his first marriage—*his* unrequited love had made it too painful.

But did his love continue to be unrequited? she wondered suddenly. His dashing off to be with a woman whom he had not seen for three years seemed distinctly odd, whereas his journey would make far more sense within the context of a current connection. Might meeting Isobel in London—when she had smiled so sweetly, kissed him and called him 'darling', Anya remembered—have prompted Garson to make an attempt to revive their relationship? Could he be wooing, and perhaps winning, the blonde all over again? Rather than restructuring his companies, had he devoted the past two months to restructuring their liaison?

But, if so, would he have come home and made such ardent love to her last night? Yes. No. Possibly. Anya twisted her wedding ring around and around her finger.

There were too many contradictions in their relationship and too many unasked questions.

But how relieved she was that she had not told Garson—the master of heartbreak—that she loved him. Mercifully, he would never know how last night, as their bodies had joined together, she had been just a breath away from saying 'I love you'. Neither would he know how she had later lain awake in the dark, gazing at him as he slept and adoring him. Anya rose to her feet. But Garson adored Isobel Dewing and had gone to her. So now she would go to bed.

Anya showered, cleaned her teeth and drew on her nightgown. Climbing into the four-poster, she lay on her stomach and yanked the pillow over her head. She pulled it close around her ears. She refused to lie awake all night, pathetically listening for the sound of the returning Maserati and thinking, thinking, thinking. She would sleep, Anya told herself determinedly, though in order to do so she would need to resort to the age-old ploy of counting sheep.

She had reached a laborious and not at all sleep-inducing one hundred and twenty, when she heard the muted swish of the bedroom door opening. Lifting the pillow off her head, Anya rolled over. She expected to see Oliver amble sleepily in, complaining of being too hot, or too cold, or thirsty, but instead a tall figure in a brown sheepskin jacket and dark trousers walked in through the shadows. She sat up, the blood rushing to her head with the shock of seeing him.

'Well, well, just look who's decided to come back. Couldn't you find the knockout Isobel?' Anya asked waspishly.

Garson came forward to bend and switch on the cream-shaded lamp which sat on the bedside table. 'I found her.' He hesitated, his expression grave. 'And I know that you're having my child.'

'So you aren't going to resurrect my supposed enticement of Roger Adlam and suggest that he might be the father?' she enquired, her voice as sharp as a razor.

He frowned. 'Of course not.'

'Why "of course"?' Anya demanded. 'Let's face it, Garson, you've never really shaken off your first idea about me—and about my sister—that we're morally unsound!'

'You're wrong,' he grated. 'When I said I understood the reason why Jennie became entangled with Luke, I meant it. As for you—hell, I know of your distaste for affairs. I know you don't sleep around.'

'True,' she snapped. 'There were only two men before you.'

'Dirk and—who?' Garson enquired curiously.

'A boy at university. But we were both playing at love and too young.' Anya paused. 'However, neither he nor Dirk *used* me.'

'I haven't used you,' he said brusquely.

'No? As I see it, I've been a convenient outlet for your frustrated desires or, to put it another way, you've exploited my desires. Whichever, I've been a substitute for Isobel.'

'Wrong again,' Garson rasped.

'Though I offered Oliver and he was the crucial factor,' Anya carried on, a mixture of anger, resentment and pain simmering inside her. 'If I hadn't had him you would never've bothered to manoeuvre me into marriage. However, this time it's *me* who makes the decisions,' she declared, with a flash of her eyes, 'and, no matter what you say or what pressure you attempt to apply, I will not—repeat *not*—terminate this baby!'

'You think I'd want you to do that?' he protested, in a voice full of outrage.

'You don't?' Anya said uncertainly.

'God Almighty, no!'

She frowned. 'But me having a child is bound to put a strain on your relationship with Isobel.'

'There isn't a relationship,' Garson said heavily.

Sitting stiff and rebellious in the pool of golden light, Anya waited for him to say more. He didn't. Instead Garson stood in silence, gazing down at her. A moment of time ticked by. And another. As his eyes started to move over her in seeming slow motion, she became conscious of how she must look. With her dark hair a foam of tousled curls, with the topaz silk nightdress clinging to her breasts, and, Anya realised, with a shoestring strap drooped fetchingly over one shoulder, she would look seductive.

She shot him a glance for confirmation and saw unconcealed desire in his eyes. Her heart pounded. Loving a man did strange things to a woman's mind, she thought, for regardless of Garson's rushing away to seek out Isobel—his beloved—she also desired him. Should she lower the other strap and let the nightgown slither down to her waist? Should she rest back on her arms and emphasise the curves of her naked breasts?

Furious with herself, Anya hooked up the strap. Her brain must be addled. Garson might still lust after her, but he did not love her—and she refused to be exploited again.

'I reckon some straight talking is long overdue,' she declared. 'I want to know why you dashed off to see Isobel this evening and I want the whole truth.'

Garson's head lifted. 'You'll have it, but if we talk here we could disturb Oliver so I suggest we go downstairs.' He strode to the door. 'I intend to have that gin and tonic, at long last. Can I get you something?'

'Er—' her throat felt parched and tense with stress '—a cup of hot chocolate.'

'You don't usually drink that.'

Anya shone him a plastic smile. 'No, but I'm pregnant—remember?'

'As if I could forget,' Garson said soberly, and disappeared.

Climbing out of bed, Anya crossed to the wardrobe. She needed a wrap, though she was damned if she would wear the negligée which he had bought her. She pulled on a pink towelling robe. It was ages old, with threads pulled in places, but it covered her completely. There was no way she could look seductive—nor want to *be* seductive—in this, Anya thought tartly as she knotted the sash.

After slipping her feet into a pair of mules, she ran a comb through her hair. She frowned at her reflection in the mirror. She had demanded that Garson tell her the whole truth about his ex-wife and yet hearing him spell out his feelings could well crucify her!

'I didn't go to see Isobel because I wanted to see her, but because I *had* to see her,' Garson began, when they were seated on the sofa in the drawing room, with their respective drinks.

'And how many other times during the past eight weeks have you *had* to see her?' Anya enquired.

'Excuse me?'

'How much of that time have you spent in London?'

'Just the occasional couple of days when I was passing through the office,' he replied, 'but you know that. You know that when I telephoned you the majority of my calls came from abroad.'

'All I know is that you said you were abroad, but you could've been in London with Isobel,' Anya declared, and suddenly felt so incensed by his homing-pigeon flight to the woman that she wanted to yell. Loud and long. 'I don't consider I look anything like her,' she said, in an abrupt veer, 'but when you bought me the underwear was it because you were attempting to re-create me in her image?'

Garson gave his head a disbelieving shake. 'You're nuts,' he said.

'So when you make love to me—' she fixed her eyes on a point somewhere beyond his shoulder '—you're not imagining that you're making love to her?'

He slammed down his glass on the coffee-table, sending the liquid splashing. 'I find that idea repulsive and obscene and unworthy of an answer! I haven't been seeing Isobel—'

'You went to see her this evening.'

'Anya, I had to get *her* to do some straight talking!' he said harshly.

'About what?' she asked, puzzled.

Garson looked at her along the length of the sofa. 'Before I explain, first I want to apologise for reacting like I did earlier and for upsetting you. God knows, I never meant to. But when you said you were pregnant it was such a shock that—' he raked the fall of dark hair back from his brow '—I lost it. In total. When you ran out, it took me a minute or two to work out why because I hadn't realised that I'd said what I was thinking out loud.' He moistened his lips. 'I didn't say the baby wasn't mine, I said it couldn't be mine.'

Anya frowned. 'What's the difference?'

His expression suddenly became drawn and haggard. 'The difference is—was—that I believed I was sterile.'

'Sterile?' It took her a moment to absorb the idea. 'But why didn't you say?'

'Because I found it so...shameful and distressing that I couldn't bring myself to talk about it.'

'You shouldn't have felt ashamed,' Anya protested. 'Sterility is a biological error—'

'I know, I know,' Garson cut in, 'and I know I was too damn proud, but that's why I told you we wouldn't have a family and never mentioned birth control. I just hoped that when nothing happened you'd gradually realise the situation, decide that Oliver filled the gap—' he bowed his head '—and find it in your heart to forgive me.'

Compassion tightened her throat. 'Oh, Garson,' she said.

'I guess it takes a special kind of genius to think problems can be solved that way,' he said, with a twisted smile. 'And it never occurred to me that you'd go on the Pill.'

'But why should you believe you were sterile?' Anya enquired.

'Because of Isobel.' He was silent and frowning for a moment, then he roused himself. 'When we got married it was agreed that we'd wait a couple of years before we had a family,' he began to explain. 'Isobel was a co-presenter on a children's programme at the time, but she reckoned there'd be no problem combining it with motherhood. In due course the two years were up and she abandoned precautions, so she said, and—zilch.'

'Isobel was still doing the children's show?'

'Yes, though what I didn't know was that she was frantically wheeling and dealing behind the scenes to get herself a job on a prime-time programme. And she did get it.'

'That's the job she's doing now?' Anya asked.

'Not quite. At the start she was one of a team of three presenters, but over the years and by various means she's managed to get rid of the other two.'

'Various means?'

'By being smarter, slicker, more determined. But also by nestling up to the producer and spreading rumours about, for instance, one of the presenters being a closet alcoholic and thus unreliable.'

Anya frowned. 'False rumours?'

'I'm afraid so. After six months had gone by, Isobel said she was worried about her failure to conceive,' Garson continued, 'and took herself off to the doctor. She told me he'd said to give it longer and another few months passed. Again she announced she was going to the doctor's, only this time she claimed to take all manner of tests, at the end of which she announced that it'd been proved the fault didn't lie with her—so it must lie with me.

'She referred to the difficulty my parents had had before conceiving Luke and pointed out, most sympathetically and with great understanding, that low fertility appeared to be a family trait.'

Anya heard the bitterness in his voice. 'Had she taken the tests?' she asked.

He shook his head. 'Isobel had never even been to see the doctor, so she confessed when I confronted her earlier this evening. Nor had she stopped taking precautions.'

'She'd lied about the whole thing and then blamed you?' Anya protested. 'That's cruel.'

Garson gave a curt nod.

'Didn't you suggest taking tests yourself to see if something could be done?' she enquired.

'Yes, but Isobel reckoned she didn't want to put me through any hassle. She very nobly declared that she was happy to forsake the idea of offspring and transfer her creative drive to her career.' Garson gave a cryptic smile. 'Which she proceeded to do with great gusto.'

'Somewhere along the way, Isobel had decided she didn't want children?'

'She admitted this evening that she'd never wanted them. That her single focus had always centred on becoming a big name in television.'

Anya's brow crimped. 'But why go through all that charade? Why not make it clear from the start that she wasn't interested in a family?'

'Because if she had she wouldn't have been sure whether or not I'd marry her.'

'And Isobel loved you,' she said flatly, thinking how much she loved him.

'I guess.' A nerve throbbed in his temple. 'But she was also keen to marry me because, me being a business whizkid, as the papers said, she visualised us socialising with the jet set, which would provide contacts she could use in her career. However, much as she tried to steer me towards the jet set, I resisted it.'

Lifting his glass, Garson took a mouthful of gin and tonic. 'Another attraction was my bankability. Whereas I've found it the devil's own job to buy you *anything*,' he said drily, 'Isobel was forever dropping hints about the beautiful gold bracelet she'd seen, or designer dress, or how her car was now two years old. Initially, I opened my wallet and obliged, but it soon occurred to me that she derived a vast amount of greedy pleasure from her acquisitions. And when we divorced the woman grabbed every last penny she could get.'

'And her behaviour is another reason why you were so quick to think that *I* was a gold-digger,' Anya said.

He pursed his lips. 'Could be,' he acknowledged.

'Would you have married Isobel if you'd known she didn't want children?' she asked.

'Yes, because I loved her. Correction, I loved the Isobel Dewing I saw, but just as your sister misread Luke's character, so I misread hers. As time went by and I realised she'd married me with an eye to furthering her career, my love started to die,' Garson continued. 'Which is why I was willing to be dissuaded from undergoing sterility tests. I wasn't sure the marriage was secure enough for kids,' he explained. 'And as it dawned on Isobel that I wasn't prepared to fraternise with "useful" people her affection for me also took a tumble.'

'Is she dating the programme controller in the hope that he might be useful?' Anya enquired.

He nodded. 'For sure.'

'But Isobel seemed so nice,' she protested.

'She is, on the surface. When they first meet her, everyone likes her. But unfortunately she has this driving ambition which dictates everything she does and means she can be ruthless.' Garson frowned. 'Leaving me to believe I was incapable of becoming a father, long after our divorce, was pretty ruthless.'

'But she confessed all this evening?'

'In frenetic detail when I buttonholed her at the studios.' He gave a dry smile. 'I was in such a white-hot rage that I think she felt that if she didn't own up and immediately I might go storming onto live television and create a national scandal.'

'So your travelling didn't play a part in your divorce?' Anya said.

He shook his head. 'I know I'm reckoned to be ultra-ambitious too, but when we first married I made a point of working nine to five and seldom went abroad. Isobel was the one who concentrated on her career, spending long hours at the studios and often going on to 'network' in the local wine bar. It was only as our relationship deteriorated and I needed an outlet for my repressed energy that I devoted so much time to business.' Garson took another mouthful of gin and tonic. 'And by repressed energy I'm referring to an unsatisfactory sex life.'

Anya looked at him in surprise. 'Unsatisfactory?' she protested. 'But we—'

'It wasn't you and me,' he said. 'I once mentioned incompatability and—well, sex didn't rate too high on the scale of pleasures with Isobel. She may've been willing to slip between the sheets if she felt a guy could be useful, but she didn't care for it.' He frowned down into his glass. 'After you and I make love, we lie together and touch and kiss, but Isobel would get up and go straight into the shower. She disliked the messiness of sex.'

'And needed to be perfect?'

Garson smiled wryly. 'Yes. Although I would've married Isobel regardless of kids, I've always wanted them,' he continued, after a moment. 'When I saw Oliver and realised Luke had fathered this great little boy and never even bothered to see him I was so angry, and so damn envious. But now—' All of a sudden his self-control went and she saw tears in his eyes. 'Anya, you're going to have a baby. Our baby,' he said, and needed to stop again to compose himself. 'It's wonderful news. I'm so happy.'

She smiled. 'And me.'

Tipping back his head, he drained his glass. 'Suppose we end this action-packed night by soaking ourselves in a warm bath before we fall into bed?'

At his words, Anya's happiness drained away. Whilst it was a huge relief to know that Garson felt nothing for Isobel, the basic flaw in their relationship still remained. He might trust her and be delighted about the baby, yet he had not mentioned loving her. So if she agreed to take up again where they'd left off wouldn't she be sliding straight back into that catastrophe for her heart and mind?

'You're scared Oliver might get to hear of our debauchery and spread the news around his school?' Garson said, when he saw her hesitation. Grinning, he pressed a finger to his lips. 'I won't snitch, I promise.'

'It's not that.' Anya plucked at a loose thread on her robe. 'I know you'll keep your word and our marriage will be permanent—even if you do go away for two months at a stretch,' she could not resist inserting. 'You're also extremely generous and please don't think I'm ungrateful. I'm not, because I always knew the score. And you're a good friend and fun to be with and—' She heard herself starting to babble and stray from the point, and swallowed in a breath. 'But I want a divorce.'

CHAPTER NINE

GARSON stared at her. 'A divorce? But—but you're having our child.'

'Yes, and I know you'd be a great father. I also know you'll think I'm being too idealistic, too picky,' Anya said, 'and, all things considered, maybe I am, but—'

'You're talking about Dirk,' he said roughly.

'Dirk?'

'You still care for the guy.'

Anya shook her head. 'I don't believe I ever cared. Not deeply.'

'But I thought Dirk was your true love,' Garson protested.

Her brow creased as her thoughts retreated to a past conversation. 'When you talked about true loves not presenting themselves too often, you were referring to him?' she enquired.

'Yes, and when I said about how you can continue to love someone, no matter how much they've hurt you.'

'This time it's you who's got things wrong,' Anya said.

Garson looked at her in confusion. 'But when you told me about your relationship with Dirk it was obvious he'd hurt you and that you still felt the pain.'

'He did. I do. But he'd hurt me because of Oliver, because of his attitude towards him.'

'Which was?' he asked, when she frowned.

'Dirk wanted me to offer Oliver up for adoption.'

Garson winced. 'Oh, God!'

'From the start, Dirk's manner with him was cool and formal, but I put it down to him not having had much to do with small children,' Anya said ruefully. 'However, as time passed, it became noticeable that he never made a single attempt to be friendly. In fact, he ignored Oliver as much as possible. I kept hoping that things would change—'

'Because you liked Dirk?'

'I liked him very much. You'd have liked him too.'

'He was nice, like Isobel?' Garson enquired.

She gave a small smile. 'Yes. But one day, after he'd started to talk about us sharing the future, he suggested I should have Oliver adopted. When I objected, Dirk said he wasn't my child and declared that he'd soon get used to a new family.'

'Oliver would've been—what, three?'

Anya nodded. 'And old enough to find the experience traumatic.'

'Extremely. But the guy must've realised how devoted you are to him,' Garson protested.

'I'd thought so. I'd also thought Dirk and I were in tune, kindred spirits, but at that point I realised he didn't know the first thing about me and I didn't know him. Or love him.'

His brows came down. 'If you don't love Dirk, why the hell do you want a divorce?' he demanded.

'Because—well, I didn't think it mattered; I believed I could handle it and maybe I could, in the short term. And maybe it's a minor carp. At least, from your point of view.' Anya knew she had started to babble again, but she could not stop. 'And, if I was someone else, it could work. I mean, you only have to look at the divorce rate in the Western world to realise that romantic marriage is a lottery-ticket deal, whereas marriages which are arranged—'

'Could you just tell me the minor carp?' Garson cut in.

'What? Oh. You don't love me,' she said, and frowned. Her voice had emerged as a miserable squeak, but why should she squeak when it was *he* who was at fault? 'You don't love me,' Anya repeated, and this time she was angry.

'I love you more than life itself,' he declared.

She slung him a suspicious look. 'You've never said you love me before.'

'Only because I believed you were still in love with Dirk,' Garson shot back. 'Why do you think I was so determined to get you to marry me?'

'Determined? Huh, you reckoned you were making a proposition, but to me it felt like a shotgun wedding!'

'Anya, I needed you,' he insisted, and his tone softened. 'I needed you because I love you so damn much.'

Joy began to pulse around her heart. 'Truly?'

'Truly, madly and for ever,' Garson declared and, much to Anya's surprise, she started to weep.

She wept with relief... and with regret that they had spent so long being mistaken about each other... and for the wonderful future which they could now share, together with Oliver and their baby.

'Don't cry,' he said, holding her close. 'I want you to be happy.'

'I am,' she told him. 'You were ruthless,' Anya said, when she had recovered and her tears had been wiped away. 'When I think of how you started to make love to me, and then stopped. You were a bastard.'

Unrepentant, Garson grinned. 'I told you there was nothing I wouldn't stoop to if there was something I wanted which I knew was right, and I knew we'd be right together. Ideal together. But do you imagine I found it easy to stop making love?' he demanded.

'You didn't?'

'It took every last ounce of my will-power, and was pure and utter hell.'

'Good!'

'But your independent streak meant I had no option but to pull out all the stops,' Garson continued defensively. 'I was terrified that if I gave you too much time to think you wouldn't agree to marry me and then—'

'Would you have broken off all contact?' Anya asked curiously.

'No. I could never've stayed away from you. It would've been impossible. And there's no way I would've kept Oliver and my folks apart, either. But I had to—'

'Trap me?'

'Anya, if you'd considered my proposition in the clear light of day you could've decided to take off and disappear and I might never have found you again,' Garson protested, then he smiled. 'But all's fair in love and war, and I was determined that when we were married I'd make you fall in love with me.'

Anya wrapped her arms around his neck. 'It happened before then,' she told him.

'You love me?'

'Don't you believe me?'

His mouth curved. 'Yes, but you've never said.'

'Only because you never said so to me. I might be independent, but I'm not so independent that I could manage to say it first,' she told him ruefully.

'So say it now.'

'I love you, I love you, I love you,' Anya declared, and Garson kissed her.

'You remember how I kissed you when we collided in the dark?' he asked. 'I never meant to and I was furious with myself, but with such a deliciously kissable mouth and those big eyes you were irresistible.'

She grinned, her mind going back. 'If I hadn't stopped things when you licked the champagne from my fingers, would you have made love to me?'

'For certain,' he said, 'though afterwards I was glad I hadn't because I really needed to explain my connection to Luke first.'

'Which was a big surprise. Like you staying away for two whole months was a surprise too,' Anya added pertly.

'It was for a reason,' Garson protested. 'I wasn't going to tell you until everything was in place, which it will be in another couple of weeks, but I've been arranging things so that I'll be able to do a good proportion of my work from here. I thought that if you use the downstairs of your cottage as your studio I could take over one of the bedrooms as my office,' he explained.

'Sounds fine to me,' she agreed delightedly.

'I've been clutching the reins too tightly and for too long, but I'm letting go. The reorganisation was more complicated than I'd anticipated, but from now on my managers will be handling most of the deals, making many of the decisions, and doing ninety per cent of the travelling.' He rubbed the tip of his nose against hers. 'While I spend my time with my beautiful wife.'

'So you'll be here when our baby is born?'

Garson placed a gentle hand on her stomach. 'Try and keep me away. But before then,' he went on seriously, 'I think we should regularise Oliver's position by both of us adopting him.'

Anya nodded. 'That's a great idea.'

Standing up, Garson drew her to her feet. 'And, to revert to my earlier one, it's bathtime,' he said.

A few minutes later he fitted himself into the end of the bath, while Anya rested back against him. A handful of fragrant rose-scented crystals had been added to the water and soap bubbles frothed around them.

'I like it,' she murmured as he lazily soaped her breasts. 'Mmm,' she said, arching her spine as his fingers slid over the glossed peaks of her nipples, 'that feels rather delicious too.'

Garson drew her closer, his thighs against her lower back. 'How about that?' he enquired.

'More than delicious . . . magnificent.'

'Flatterer,' he said, laughing, and reached for a towel.

Although the urgency of their need meant that their bodies were damp when they climbed into the four-poster bed, the heat of passion quickly dried them. As hands touched, stroked, caressed, their breathing quickened and their desire grew.

But this time it's different, Anya thought mistily as she guided him inside her. This time the feeling is deeper and surer, because now we know that we love each other.

'That was the bestest,' Garson murmured afterwards as they drifted in sweet euphoria.

'The very bestest,' Anya agreed.

He brushed his lips against hers. 'I realise it's rather late in the day for a proposal,' he said, 'but please, my darling, will you marry me and live with me for ever and ever?'

'I will,' she vowed.

Anya snuggled closer and, as stars sparkled in the black velvet of the sky, she fell asleep, entwined in the arms of the man whom she had once considered the master of heartbreak, but whom she now knew to be the master of love.

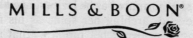

MILLS & BOON®

Anne Mather Collection

This summer Mills & Boon brings you a powerful
collection of three passionate love stories from
an outstanding author of romance:

Tidewater Seduction
Rich as Sin
Snowfire

576 pages of passion, drama and
compelling story lines.

Available: August 1996

MILLS & BOON®

Next Month's Romances

♡

Each month you can choose from a wide variety of romance with Mills & Boon. Below are the new titles to look out for next month in our two new series Presents and Enchanted.

Presents™

WOMAN TO WED?	Penny Jordan
MISTRESS MATERIAL	Sharon Kendrick
FINN'S TWINS!	Anne McAllister
AFTER HOURS	Sandra Field
MR LOVERMAN	Mary Lyons
SEDUCED	Amanda Browning
THE FATHER OF HER CHILD	Emma Darcy
A GUILTY AFFAIR	Diana Hamilton

Enchanted™

A KISS FOR JULIE	Betty Neels
AN INNOCENT CHARADE	Patricia Wilson
THE RIGHT HUSBAND	Kay Gregory
THE COWBOY WANTS A WIFE!	Susan Fox
PART-TIME WIFE	Jessica Hart
BRIDES FOR BROTHERS	Debbie Macomber
GETTING OVER HARRY	Renee Roszel
THREE LITTLE MIRACLES	Rebecca Winters

Available from WH Smith, John Menzies, Volume One, Forbuoys, Martins, Woolworths, Tesco, Asda, Safeway and other paperback stockists.

One to Another

A year's supply of Mills & Boon® novels— absolutely FREE!

Would you like to win a year's supply of heartwarming and passionate romances? Well, you can and they're FREE! Simply complete the missing word competition below and send it to us by 28th February 1997. The first 5 correct entries picked after the closing date will win a year's supply of Mills & Boon romance novels (six books every month—worth over £150). What could be easier?

PAPER	**B A C K**	WARDS
ARM		MAN
PAIN		ON
SHOE		TOP
FIRE		MAT
WAIST		HANGER
BED		BOX
BACK		AGE
RAIN		FALL
CHOPPING		ROOM

Please turn over for details of how to enter ☞

How to enter...

There are ten missing words in our grid overleaf. Each of the missing words must connect up with the words on either side to make a new word—e.g. PAPER-BACK-WARDS. As you find each one, write it in the space provided, we've done the first one for you!

When you have found all the words, don't forget to fill in your name and address in the space provided below and pop this page into an envelope (you don't even need a stamp) and post it today. Hurry—competition ends 28th February 1997.

Mills & Boon® One to Another
FREEPOST
Croydon
Surrey
CR9 3WZ

Are you a Reader Service Subscriber?   Yes ❑   No ❑

Ms/Mrs/Miss/Mr _____

Address _____

_____

_____ Postcode _____

One application per household.

C496
A